EDGES

An ART OF EROS Novel, Book 2

Copyright © 2018 by Kenzie MaCallan

978-0-9973492-3-8

Published by Steel Butterfly Press

This is a work of fiction. Names, characters, places and incidents
are either the product of the author's imagination or are used fictitiously, and any resemblance to actual persons, living or dead, business establishments, events or locales is entirely coincidental.

Printed in the USA.

Editing services provided by Lawrence Editing

Cover Design © 2017 Louisa Maggio

Cover model: Garry Turner Instagram@ gtrain_pro

Interior Format

EDGES

AN *ART OF EROS* NOVEL

BOOK 2

KENZIE MACALLAN

Steel Butterfly Press

You have nothing to fear but fear itself.
Just let go.
Feel the fear and do it anyway.

CHAPTER 1

Leigha Luccenzo stood stock-still in the doorway and gaped at the destruction of her apartment. *Sydney.* Goddamn her! That woman didn't take no for an answer. She didn't need this after months of family drama. Her anxiety spiked as her heart pounded in her ears. Papers sprayed out all over. The drawers to the end tables were ripped out of their places. *God no.* The bookshelf once full of her favorite photograph binders, stood vacant, lying in a scrambled heap on the floor. *What for?*

Her breath shortened and hands trembled. Her fists clenched into tight balls. Metal-framed photos lay askew on the wall. She gasped at the sight of her prized ceramic and glass pig collection scattered all over.

Anger melted to hurt as the chaos blurred through tears brimming in her eyes. More than anyone, her ex-lover had understood Leigha's need for order, for control. How could she? Better yet, why? Was she looking for something? She sucked in her breath to keep her emotions in check. The sight before her pulled on the thread that bound her, nearing its breaking point. The late afternoon light caught the pieces of shattered glass matching her heart at the sight of her home.

She broke out in a cold sweat. Her body shook of its own volition. This couldn't be happening. The ghost of violation snuck into her soul again as pieces of her nightmare bled their way back into her life. They threatened to destroy her. She couldn't catch her breath. Heaviness wrapped around her body. *Focus. Focus!* She had to hold it together.

The path of carnage went from the living room into the back bedroom. Talking her way through it, she convinced herself it was just stuff. Right? So why did it feel like something had been torn from her? She compartmentalized like a champ and would handle this like everything else. This event would have its own little box.

Her need for control snapped back in place like couture armor serving to mask the insecurity underneath. Her soul bristled, wanting to be free of its confined edges. Freedom was a luxury she lost years ago. She couldn't remember when things had changed. As long as she maintained control, nothing could hurt her. A harsh sigh of acceptance left her as she contemplated her reality. Loneliness consumed her, unable to break free of her hemmed in existence.

But defeat was not an option.

She pulled her shoulders back and closed the door, carefully stepping over shattered Waterford vases, broken one-of-a-kind Tiffany lamps, and overturned furniture. With every broken thing, the tear grew. She bent down to pick up one of her precious pigs but stopped short. The scene shouldn't be disturbed. God knows she watched enough crime shows to know the routine.

Her hands shook as she pulled her cell phone from its pocket in her purse. She missed the buttons several times. The need to get a hold of her sister overwhelmed her. Finally, her sister's phone rang.

"It–it's me." She held her palm to her forehead, trying to steady herself.

"What's wrong?" Alarm sounded in Mara's voice.

"Someone broke into my apartment. I need you to come over. Is Mac with you?"

Mac, Mara's boyfriend, was the only one she trusted in this situation.

"Yes. I'll call Raquelle."

"Please," she whispered. She needed both of her sisters, the bookends to their trio.

"Are you okay? You're starting to scare me," Mara begged.

"I don't know. You need to see it for yourself. Please hurry." She hoped she didn't sound too desperate.

Their conversation gave her slight relief. Her inner battle raged to regain her composure before her sisters came over. She was their rock and wasn't about to let them see her crumble.

The minutes ticked by like molasses while she stood in the middle of the wreckage. Her head swam with thoughts of why Sydney chose to destroy her apartment. They hadn't even been that serious. Maybe she assumed too much given what had happened in Mexico.

She constantly checked her cell phone for the time. Where were they? They lived a block away.

The knock at the door popped her out of her spiraling thoughts. Her cell phone dropped from her hand. She walked to the door and relief washed over her as she looked through the peephole. Mara's worried eyes looked back at her. She fell apart on the inside, but she couldn't let her sister see it.

"Thank God you're here."

Mac and Mara stepped inside, surveying the damage.

Mara's eyes went wide as she gasped. "Leigha, what happened?" She whispered as if she didn't want to further add to the unrest.

"I have no idea. This is what I came home to. I think this is Sydney's handiwork." Having a summer fling with Sydney suddenly seemed like a bad idea. Another bad decision in the romance department.

Mac scanned the scene, surveying the damage. "Don't touch anything. I'm calling NYPD." His Scottish accent rolled over his words, making him hard to understand. He left to make a call in the kitchen.

She covered her mouth with a shaking hand, trying to keep her emotions at bay. Mara enveloped her like a fine piece of china. She accepted the comfort, her inner self unraveling with every passing minute. Lost in her own thoughts with questions of who and why, she jumped as Raquelle entered the room.

"Holy shit!" Raquelle stood in the doorway with eyes wide. "What a mess. What the hell happened?"

"Thank you, Captain Obvious," Mara shot back. "We're trying to figure that out. Come in and shut the door."

Raquelle stepped in and gave Leigha a tight, Italian hug.

"Be careful. Mac says we can't disturb anything," Mara said to the youngest of the Luccenzo brood.

Mac came back in the room wearing tight lines around his eyes. "I called my contact at NYPD. They're on their way. Leigha, why don't you walk with me as I survey the rest of the apartment? Let me know if anything's missing," he said as he led the way to the master bedroom.

She stumbled next to him, unsure she wanted to see what lay ahead. "I'm pretty sure this is Sydney's handy work. What I can't figure out is why." Her voice shook.

Mac responded with an unconvincing hum.

He examined the mess, his brows furrowed while snapping pictures with his phone. They entered the bedroom where things appeared untouched. He stopped and turned to her.

"Why don't you go back to your sisters in the living room? I can take it from here."

"Why is this room spotless? If you're going to destroy someone's apartment, why not go all the way?" Her voice sounded strained in her own ears.

He ignored her comment as he pressed buttons on his phone. "I need you to go back to your sisters. I got this."

Her ability to fight drained from her. Taking a couple of steps out of the room, she stopped when she overheard part of Mac's conversation.

"Sean, it's Mac. We've got a situation we need to consider as part of our case."

Sean Knight was one of Mac's bosses. What could this have to do with any case? Mac, an ex–MI6, a British spy, worked at the private security firm of MBK Global Security.

"My girlfriend's sister's apartment has been broken into. Looks like they were searching for something specific. This might be the work of the Russians." His words were tight. "I don't know what they want with Leigha."

Her mind spun. The only Russians she knew about were the ones who'd killed Mara's husband in Mexico. What could the Russians want with her? Her head pounded as her thoughts bore down on her. She couldn't stand to hear any more as she made her way back to her sisters.

Raquelle sat perched on the arm of the couch, talking to Mara, whose furrowed brows reflected her own worry. They both turned her way as Mara spoke up.

"Is everything okay? Was anything taken?"

"I can't tell. I'll know tomorrow when I start to put things in order." She crossed her arms, hugging herself as confusion dissolved into worry.

Mac came back in the room. "Ladies, we need to go. Leigha, you're staying with Mara and me, so you need to go gather your things." The urgency in Mac's voice left no room for questions.

Mara put her hands on her hips. "Since when are you and I living together? I'm quite capable of taking care of my sister on my own, thank you."

He held Mara's shoulders and his eyes softened. "I made a promise to watch over you and that extends to your sisters. So you need to accept we're living together until this blows over. I can't give you the details, but it may be tied to the things that happened in Cancun. You need to trust me."

Raquelle piped in, "Please tell me that son-of-bitch husband of hers is really dead. Because this doesn't make any sense."

He gave her a hard stare. "Yes. Brock is dead. But you don't have all the pieces to the puzzle and neither do I. Let's leave it at that."

Leigha spoke up. "Why can't this just be Sydney getting back at me? Why does it have to be part of any case or the Russians?" She crossed her arms in front of her, hoping to hide her shattered nerves.

He let go of Mara and turned to her. His eyes scanned her face. "Leave it to you to listen in."

"I have a right to know what's going on." Anger bubbled to the surface. She refused to be left in the dark.

"I don't know yet. What you don't know is that Sydney has gone dark, missing. So I don't think this was Sydney." His face fell at the worry of his ex MI6 partner.

Leigha, dazed by the revelation, headed to her bedroom to gather her belongings. She rushed to her nightstand, making sure she left with one of her most treasured items, a picture in a plastic bag. Relief flooded over her as she untaped the flat bag from the top inside of her nightstand. The photo, shot at a distance, pictured her father and another man. They were laughing and carrying on as if they were brothers. She didn't remember a time when her father laughed with her. There had always been a distance between them she couldn't explain.

Her thumb rubbed over it, wondering about the other man's story. He intrigued her, yet she never saw him again. She kept this photo separate from the others, as a reminder of how much she didn't really know about her father. Did the other man have the answers to questions she was too afraid to ask?

The photo would go with her. She packed a few things, from clothes to toiletries, and returned to the living room with a small suitcase. "I'm ready when you are."

Raquelle stood, ready to go. "Tomorrow we'll call a cleaning service to come in and clean this mess up." She waved her hands around, dismissing the event.

Leigha screeched. "I don't want anyone near my apartment. Do you understand me? No one. I will clean it up myself. I need to put things back where they belong, in their proper place."

"I'm sorry." Raquelle recoiled. "I wasn't thinking. I'm sorry." She walked over to hug her. "My mind has been everywhere lately. I feel a little ADD."

That was an understatement.

Mara glared at Raquelle. "How about if we help you put it together tomorrow? You can tell us exactly where everything should go."

"Yeah, that sounds good." Her hand shook as she ran it along the top of her head, tucking stray hairs back into her secured bun.

As they turned to leave, NYPD showed up. Mac met with them in the hallway, out of earshot.

He returned, motioning to Leigha. "The police

need to speak with you."

The cop standing with him looked stone-faced, as if it were another boring call.

He held out his hand. "I'm Officer Reilly. Mac filled me in on Sydney. Is there anything else you can tell me? Has anyone been following you?"

"No. I don't think so. At least not that I'm aware of." She held her hands together to stop the shaking. Maybe this was about a case and not about Sydney after all. How long had she been missing?

His eyes searched her face, analyzing her response. He asked her several more questions as they went through the apartment.

"Thank you. We'll be in touch if we need you. You'll be able to return tomorrow." He gave her a half-hearted smile.

Her sisters and Mac stood whispering in the hallway.

"You don't have to whisper. I'm not made of glass. I can take whatever you have to say." Her words covered the truth as jumpy nerves skated under her skin.

"We're worried about you and trying to piece things together." Raquelle gave her a hug. Holding her by the shoulders, she said, "I'll talk to you tomorrow."

Mara squeezed her hand as they walked to the elevator and whispered, "Are you going to be all right? I've never seen you like this."

"It's all too much sometimes." The words caught in her throat. Her life seemed like a beautiful stained glass window. The cut pieces made to fit together perfectly. The edges were neat and secured. Someone had punched a hole in her window. The jagged pieces cut her forcing her to feel things she wanted to ignore.

Mara peered at her with concerned eyes and put her arm around her shoulders. "Let's go home and I'll make you some tea."

The tables had turned in an instant. After so many years of being the pillar for everyone around her, she needed support. She fell against Mara's shoulder, her mind and body tired from the day's events and warring emotions. As they walked to Mara's apartment, Mac flanked her on the street side in a gesture of protection.

Leigha sank into the soft brown leather couch with tea cupped in her hands to warm and steady them. Mac made the right call about her coming to stay with Mara. Her hands had stopped trembling. She gazed into the dark tea. The night's violation reminded her of her days as a model. Hands would slip to areas they didn't belong while fitting a garment. She posed as a living doll for them to play with as they wished. A tremor raced through her at the memory. That was one of the reasons she got out of modeling.

Mac sat down across from her, frowning and rubbing the scar above his eye. "I hate to do this, but I have to ask you some questions. Can you handle it right now?"

"I'm fine." She continued to stare at her teacup.

"Normally, I wouldn't butt into your personal business, but I have to ask about your relationship with Sydney. What happened?" He shifted uncomfortably in the chair. The worry in his eyes led onto the fact that there was more to the Sydney angle.

"I started seeing Sydney when we got back from Cancun. She was different and fun. We had a summer fling, of sorts, but it wasn't working for me anymore, so I broke it off. She tried to talk me into staying, contacting me several times. I never returned her calls." She shrugged. "When I'm done with someone, I'm done." She clamped her lips tightly.

"When was the last time she tried to contact you?"

"About two weeks ago. I think. I've been really busy lately." Had it been that long?

"Is anything missing from the apartment that you could see?" His eyes never left her face.

"I don't think so, but I won't know until I clean up. Sydney never left anything at my apartment."

"No. She wouldn't. You never leave a trail as an operative." Something flickered in his eyes and quickly left.

Her hands tightened around her cup. She wasn't sure she wanted the answer to her next question. "When did she go missing?"

"About two weeks ago." His voice was gruff.

The air became heavy with worry.

"Sydney didn't break into my apartment, did she?"

"No."

"Why is anyone after me? Is it the Russians or someone else?" Her thoughts went back to Cancun. They had found out that Mara's husband, Brock, had deceived her for their entire marriage and sexually abused her. He used her to climb the ladder and made off with millions of the Russians' money. Leigha tried to connect those dots, but they didn't seem to lead back to her.

"It was a professional job. There is no visible break-in. I can't be sure it wasn't the Russians, but I'm not willing to take any chances. I'm putting a detail on you starting tomorrow."

She raised her voice. "No. I spent my whole life having bodyguards. We don't even know who did this."

"Do you know why your father had so many bodyguards around you? It seems odd for an artist." He didn't miss a beat, as though it were something he had thought about for a while.

Her thoughts were starting to make a web that she may never get out of. She sighed. "I don't know. I never thought to ask." Her head hit the back of the couch as she stared at the ceiling.

He reached out and softly covered her hand. "Thank you, Leigha. I know this is hard for you, but this is helpful."

"Do you think Sydney is tied to the Russians?" Her heart held disappointment.

"Not sure yet, but I'll let you know." He got up and turned away quickly, hiding his face.

CHAPTER 2

*L*eigha's childhood home in Greenwich grew wisteria that wound its way around a structure, pulling it down. Years later the wisteria won out. Her nightmares wound around her, dragging her to a dark place, but she refused to let them break her.

My eyes are heavy. I can't focus. Everything is covered in red. There's heavy breathing in my ear. I'm thrashing around trying to escape, but my arms and legs are like dead weight. I want to cry out but can't catch my breath. Someone keeps talking to me. I hear my name over and over again and something about lingerie. Drifting in and out, I'm trying to hold on to the cliff of consciousness. He's in control, taking my free will as I slip away.

"Leigha, Leigha, wake up! You're dreaming." Mara stood over her but didn't touch her.

Bolting upright in bed, she gasped. Sweat covered her body as her nightshirt clung to her. She shook her head, trying to rid herself of the dream. Her fingers twisted in the sheets. She suspected the return of her nightmares came from Mara's confessional of spousal abuse. One thing after another seemed to be testing her perfect little world.

"What happened?" Her lungs struggled to take in air. She needed to know how much Mara had heard.

"You were thrashing around and calling out. Are you all right? What's going on?" Mara's face filled with anguish.

She had never told her sisters about her nightmares. The memories of the event came to her in fragments. The sharpness of the pieces cut away at her.

"What did I say?"

"I couldn't make it out." Curiosity flared in Mara's eyes.

"I'm all right. I think seeing the apartment in disarray upset me more than I expected." She stared her sister straight in the eye. Lying to cover up the truth had become second nature.

Mara hugged her. "Okay. Let me know if you need anything. Try to get some sleep."

"Thank you." She tried to smile.

"Tomorrow we'll clean up your place and put it back together the way you want it." Mara squeezed her hand and left, shutting the door behind her.

Changing her sweat soaked sleepwear, she prayed sleep would take her over before the nightmare came back. She needed to piece together the dream so it made sense. Why was her unconscious holding back? She wanted her life back. When did being in control start meaning so much? The questions haunted her as she struggled to seek answers. The nightmare may hold the answers.

A restless night's sleep made her head heavy. Her muscles ached like she'd run a marathon. She scrolled through her contacts on her cell phone to call Chloe, her assistant.

"Hey, I need you to cancel all my appointments for today. Something's come up I need to take care of."

"Something's wrong. You don't sound like yourself. What's going on?" Chloe read her like a book.

"There are some things I need to take care of at my apartment, that's all," she stated in a casual air.

"Is there anything I can do to help?" Chloe's voice carried an undercurrent of many questions.

She knew if she hid it from her she would grow more suspicious. "If you want to come by, Mara and I are going to be there. I could use an extra set of hands." Chloe would serve as a buffer between her and potential arguments with her sister.

"Let me reschedule your day. I'll be over later." Chloe clicked off.

She threw the phone on the bed and it bounced off hitting the floor. Holding her head in her hands, dread clawed at her with the thought of going back to the apartment. She clasped her hands together, praying she could hold herself together long enough to gather up the unruly living space.

Dressed in jeans and a sweater, she made her way to the kitchen. Mac and Mara sat in silence, moving their food around their plates.

"Good morning." She pasted on one of her model smiles to present a confident, nothing's wrong front.

Mara stood and gave her a hug. She hugged

her back but released Mara quickly, fearing the emotions would race to the surface and she'd fall apart.

Mara leaned back to look at her. "How are you this morning?"

"I feel a little better. Thanks for last night. I didn't realize how much all this would affect me." Her chest ached admitting her fear.

"We're going to find who did this and why." Mac sounded certain as always. "I'm off to work so I can do that." He reached out his hand for Mara.

"I'll be right back. Help yourself to anything you want." Mara got up to grab his hand.

Damn it. She wanted someone to hold her hand and tell her it would be all right. Just once she wanted to the one someone wanted. Her body lacked energy collapsing in a chair at the table. She yearned for not having to worry about everyone else. Someone to hand it all over to.

The quiet murmurings and Mara's giggles traveled down the hallway, teasing her. Mara and her Highlander had a special bond she longed for. She pushed down the sadness of what she missed in her life. Other things took precedence. She fought to stay on task.

She and Mara spent most of the day putting her apartment back together. Mara followed her directions tentatively making suggestions. She appreciated the effort her sister put into taking directions from her. Restoring her order was paramount and required all her focus.

Raquelle showed up later in the day along with Chloe. She swept into the room, waiting for the spotlight of their eyes to find her. "So how's the clean-up going, girls? Anything I can do to help like call a cleaning service? It's not too late, even at this hour."

Chloe seemed unfazed by the amount of stuff on the floor. Leigha waited for the questions that never came.

"Nice of you to show up. We don't need a cleaning service, thank you." Mara didn't look at Raquelle.

Raquelle eased into her apology. "I'm sorry. I had some important appointments today, some of which could be real career boosters for me."

Ice covered Leigha's response. "Well, it's not all about you all the time."

Raquelle's shoulders sagged. "I know. Things have been a little crazy lately. How can I help?"

"You can start with that huge pile of pictures on the table. You're always good at putting stuff in chronological order." Leigha noticed that the most damage had been done to her binders of photographs. What did her pictures have to do with anything?

Raquelle made her way over to the pile. "This is a shitload of pictures. I probably won't get through them tonight. Let's order in and have a girls' night."

Leigha rolled her eyes. The ringleader had spoken. When it came to making any plan into a party, Raquelle was the go-to girl.

Chloe stopped picking up the ceramic pigs off the floor and with a strange look of concern said, "Leigha, you have an appointment at the studio I won't be able to cancel tonight."

She waved her hand in the air, dismissing the comment. "I can't go in tonight. There's too much to do. Nothing's so important it can't wait. Reschedule for first thing tomorrow morning."

"Okay. I need to make some calls." Chloe's eyes went blank as she excused herself to the back room. Something seemed off.

Raquelle sorted the photos and Leigha and Mara joined her. Going through the photos, they reminisced over their youth, from growing up in Greenwich to summer vacations in Asbury Park, New Jersey.

Raquelle made a comment that caught Leigha's attention. "It seems odd there are a lot of photos of Leigha and Mama. But where's Papa? Look at this one." She laughed.

Mara chimed in, "It's your keen eye of a portrait artist at work. Maybe those shots were taken during a time when Papa traveled a lot." She sighed. "Who's kidding who? He always traveled." Mara's voice held a hint of bitterness.

Silence fell over them, contemplating the truth about their father's absence. They each had their own axe to grind with him.

"I used to take pictures of him all the time even when he didn't know it. Maybe it was my way of feeling close to him." The questions about her father's distance went unresolved for her even after all this time.

Chloe came back in the room a little ruffled. "Well, looks like I rescheduled your meeting to first thing tomorrow morning." She gave a slight smile.

Mara's phone rang with the ringtone

"Headturner" by Joss Stone. A goofy grin spread across her face, making it obvious who was on the other end. She hurried off, taking the call in the back bedroom.

They continued to clean, righting lamps and frames, piecing together her pig collection and gathering papers.

A few minutes later, Mara walked back in the kitchen still talking on the phone. Her giddiness gone, replaced by agitation. "Yes, I got it. She's coming home with me. You don't have to repeat yourself. I'll see you at my place." She clicked off, blowing out a breath. "God, he can be so over the top alpha sometimes."

"What's going on?" Leigha said absentmindedly as she held glass fragments in her hand.

"Mac wants you to come home with me again. He doesn't have a grip on who did this and needs to set up the new security system." Mara looked at her for approval.

She still felt out of sorts. Between the break-in, the nightmares, and Chloe being weird, she would at least be safe at Mara's apartment. She needed comfort amidst the storm, praying the nightmare would stay away. "Okay. Another night at your place might do me some good."

Mara's and Raquelle's faces registered shock at her easy agreement to go home with Mara.

They finished cleaning up. There would be no girls' sleepover. A small amount of relief came over Leigha at the sight of her apartment coming back to order. She thanked everyone, realizing they came for moral support as much as anything else.

Darkness blanketed the city as they left the apartment building. Everyone said their goodbyes and went their separate ways.

"I need to text Mac and let him know we're on our way." Mara's head bent down as her fingers flew over the screen. They walked arm in arm up the street.

Mac waited for them on the outside steps. He adored her sister. He seemed to always sense Mara's presence and zero in on her. He walked over and gave her a hug and a kiss. "Leannan, how was your day?" His Scottish pet name for her meaning sweetheart rolled off his tongue.

"Fine. But I can tell by the glint in your eye, you've been up to something." Mara smiled at his boyish charm.

He beamed. "I made us dessert."

"You cook too?" Leigha interjected.

Smart, handsome, protective and he could add cook to his list. Was it possible to clone him? She could use someone to cook for her.

"Let's not get carried away. He's learning to cook. There have been some foods that would be considered lethal." Mara smirked.

"Hey, give a Highlander credit, would you?" he responded, putting on an affected Scottish brogue.

Mara and Mac led the way up to the apartment. Mara leaned into him for support and he never wavered. Who had she ever leaned on for support? No one. There wasn't one person she could hand it to.

Her sister had found her forever with someone who would stick with her through thick and thin. Being in their presence wouldn't make it rub off on her. She would have to dig deeper and unearth the self that she buried many years ago. She ached to have someone to count on with seamless effort.

After a delicious dinner of chicken parmesan, they all sat down in the living room as Mac presented them with his chocolate molten cake. He sliced into it and the liquid oozed from the center.

"So is this Betty or Duncan?" Mara said between bites.

"Duncan. I had to go with the Scotsman." He smiled.

After they finished his masterpiece, Mara excused herself to clean up the kitchen. Leigha seized the opportunity to talk to Mac. "I noticed they focused on my collection of pictures. If I saw it, then you saw it too."

"Aye, I did notice." Weariness set in as his shoulders sagged.

"Why do you think it's the Russians?" Leigha pressed him for answers.

"The break-in was way too clean. It was either a professional job or someone has the key and code to your security system."

"If this is the Russians, are they looking for pictures of Cancun? If so, they should have started with that binder. But all the binders had been rifled through. What does it mean?" Leigha sat on the edge of the chair as her leg bounced up and down.

"I have no idea what it all means. I know the Russians didn't want Brock to talk, which is one of the reasons he got killed. Is it possible you took a picture of someone you shouldn't have?" He pressed his fingertips together in a steeple.

"Not that I know of. But then again, I tend to take pictures of everything." Something niggled at her, but she couldn't put her finger on it. "Does all of this have anything to do with Sydney missing?"

He locked his eyes with hers as if he were debating telling her something. "It might. I want you to watch your back. Be more aware of your surroundings and where you go at night."

Coldness crept up her arms as more questions without answers swirled in her head.

CHAPTER 3

Her morning revelation was that she needed to share her nightmare with Mara. There would be relief in having her sister know all the pieces of her fractured life.

She spoke softly, "I need to talk to you about the other night."

"Please do. I want to help you. You seem so frazzled and then you shutdown." Mara motioned for her to sit down on the couch.

"I've been having nightmares off and on for a while now." She hugged her legs to her chest. "They have gotten worse since we came back from Mexico." She stopped as she dug her fingers into her knees.

Mara took her hands and held them. "Whatever it is, I can take it. You and Raquelle were so supportive when I told you about Brock and his abuse. It can't be worse than that."

"That's just it. I don't know what they are about." She handed over a piece of herself.

Mara frowned at her. "What do you mean? You don't remember them?"

"They come to me in fragments. Everything is

always in red. Do you think my dream is trying to tell me I killed someone?" Her chest tightened as she verbalized her deepest fear. Tears pooled in her eyes.

Her sister sat still, taking in this new piece of information. "What the hell makes you think you killed someone?" Her breath barely escaped to form words.

The tears sitting at bay crested as she bit her lower lip. She yanked her hands away from Mara's. "What else could it mean? In my dream, I'm struggling with someone. I don't know who and then I wake up. It scares the shit out of me."

"Come here." Mara pulled her into a hug and rocked her back and forth until she stopped crying.

"I'm sorry. I don't mean to put this all on you," she said through sniffles.

"Don't you dare apologize. That's what sisters are for." Mara gripped her harder.

Telling Mara this much was all she could bear in the moment. She tried to force a smile, but her soul refused to fake it.

"I need to go home and try to put the pieces together."

Mara nodded, but the worry never left her eyes. She let her go to put her suitcase together.

Making her way through the lobby, she hesitated outside the apartment building. The crowded street full of strangers made her heed Mac's warning. She glanced over her shoulder several times, looking for anyone who might be following her.

She ran up the front stairs of her building, passing the doorman without a hello. As she approached the elevator doors, she reached out to stop them. She noticed an unfamiliar man inside and pulled her hand away. "Sorry, I'll take the next one." Jitters of insecurity tugged at her.

She entered her apartment and leaned against the locked door. Order and clean lines greeted her. A sigh of relief came over her at the sight of almost everything in its place.

Her suitcase dragged behind her to the bedroom. She opened the nightstand drawer to put the picture back in place. Contentment spread through her body, but deathly quiet hung in the apartment. A reminder of her empty life.

She dropped her suitcase on the floor and plopped down on the bed. The last couple of days welled up. Tears freed themselves, making a path down her cheeks. Sobbing uncontrollably, she could only hold herself together for so long. Even with all the objects back in place, the hollow space in her soul couldn't be filled. Her life used to be so carefree, lacking the tight binds that took her freedom.

She wiped the wetness from her cheeks, resolving to push through the feelings of being unwanted, to the nightmares and the break-in. Her shoulders curled forward and her head hung. She contemplated not going to work. But that wasn't going to happen. She clung to her daily routine for stability.

Digging deep, she needed to find the energy to move forward. Photographs weren't going to take themselves. Work gave her an escape. She could bury herself there and distract herself from the world within her. Routine was the clock she lived by.

Every morning included a run in the park. Running had a peaceful rhythm to it like a meditation with the same mantra chanted over and over again. The pattern of the steady movement of her legs, the pumping of her arms and the air burning through her lungs became part of her order. A reminder she was alive. This was where she felt truly free.

She dressed for work, slipping on a light tan leather jacket to protect her from the chilled air. Her life played out like a bad movie trailer. The same routine repeated itself every day. She took the subway to Tribeca whizzing by graffiti splayed on the underground walls. The artist in her appreciated the creative outlet. Young souls who wanted to be heard as subway passengers flew by their messages. Bright-colored displays were passionate and desperate. Her passion and color seemed to have vanished years ago.

On the street, she passed by all the familiar faces of the vendors getting ready for the day. The streets started to come to life after a sleepless slumber. The quiet intensified her hollowness. She had missed the party even in the city that never sleeps. A pit sat in her stomach. She couldn't shake the feeling that she missed an important fragment of her life.

Her building came into view. She dreaded the ride in the old elevator. But she didn't have the energy for the stairs. Her knuckles turned white as she gripped the bars of the freight elevator grinding its way to the top floor. Her slice of heaven had become the photography studio. The insulated space held the quiet, except for the soft step of her shoes on spotless wood floors.

She peeled off her jacket, dumping it on a small modern deep red chair. As she took in a deep breath she was thankful the area had remained untouched. Everything was in its proper place from lighting to furniture, backdrops and her special shelf of miniature pigs.

Pigs. She loved them, appreciating their little round bodies and big, smart eyes. Her odd attachment to Wilbur from *Charlotte's Web* began the first time her mother read the book to her. She became fascinated by the fact that Wilbur was unwanted yet spared. Her mama had caught on to her affinity, giving her miniature pigs as gifts for special occasions. Each pig had a name. They all held special meaning for her, except for the broken one she left as a reminder of her past. Her hand clutched the front of her shirt. Something about it brought so much pain.

She crossed the studio and passed the dark room. A chill coursed down her spine. What was it about that room? She struggled to remember why, but it continued to elude her. Her remedy for soothing nerves could be found in a cup of white tea as she grabbed her favorite cup from the cabinet.

She carried her calming tincture and gazed out the spotless windows, trying to forget the clues of her past. Best to give it a rest for now. Her view from the top floor of the warehouse in Battery Park overlooked the dreary Hudson River. She always looked for changes in the horizon. The colors remained constant, but the hues changed daily. Tired buildings lined up across the river appeared to be holding each other up so not a sliver of light could find its way through. The warm light of the rising sun sparkled off the windows, making the buildings look like ancient dusty paper covered in gold glitter. The brightness of the sun couldn't lighten the murky water or add dimension to the skyline. Her daily mirror. She didn't care for the reflection, as her life seemed to close in on her.

Her mind went back to when she bravely told her sisters about her plans to explore things with Sydney.

"You go, girl! If I were into pussy, I would hit that too. She's stunning!" Raquelle had given her a high five, bringing attention to them in the crowded midtown restaurant. She always loved to show off her wild side.

Mara had rolled her eyes, smiling blissfully. "I want you to be happy. I want you to find the perfect someone for you." She wanted everyone to be as happy as she was with Mac, the man who'd saved her life.

Leigha felt that pang of want every time Mara spoke about her relationship with Mac.

She had responded to Mara's love-induced high. "Well, I don't know where all this is going to go, but I need to explore it. I've become so out of touch with my body and myself. Maybe this is what I need to make me happy in a relationship. Please don't tell Mama and Papa. They won't understand."

Their parents lived by the rules of old world Italy. Her newfound lifestyle wouldn't please them.

When it came to Sydney the learning curve was

huge. She taught her things about her body and the toys that could bring her joy. Sydney was quite knowledgeable when it came to how to please a woman. She knew the workings of a woman's body, making her come eighteen ways to Sunday.

She snapped out of her reverie at the sound of the elevator grinding to a stop as the grate rolled up. Her nerves were jumpy. Her hand shook, rattling the cup and saucer. She scanned the room, looking for a weapon of any kind. The clicking of shoes on the hardwood floors signaled Chloe's promptness. The breath she held escaped in a rush. She turned to her assistant and straightened her back.

Chloe said, "I see someone busted out some color today."

"I'm getting there. See the blue shirt? It counts as a color," she spoke softly.

"And a good morning to you, sunshine," Chloe chirped as she entered the kitchen area. "How are you today?" She stopped. Worry covered her face. "You look like you had a rough night. What's up? Is the nightmare back again?"

"Yeah. I can't get a grip on it. It's still in pieces and parts." She peered down into her teacup, looking for the tealeaves to give her some answers. "I told Mara about them. I feel like I can't leave her in the dark given what she shared with me about Brock. It actually felt good to share it with her."

"Do you want to talk about it? Tell me some of the details?" Chloe's voice held understanding and compassion.

She avoided reliving her personal hell. "No.

Why rehash the same thing over and over again?" Her thumb circled the top of the cup. "I like Mara and Mac together. I would love to find someone I have chemistry with, who lights my fire so to speak. For once, it would be nice to be wanted by someone I want as well. But at this point I need to put my love life on hold. It seems as though I'm not compatible with anyone." Longing tugged at her heart as she choked back her words.

"Ah, you want what Mara has. I don't blame you one bit. I want what Mara has. Everyone wants what Mara has. Mac's a wonderful guy. When I came to the big city I thought I would blend right in. That it would be easier to find someone out here than in the Midwest. But it hasn't been easy." Chloe's pin straight black hair fell in front of her flawless pink face, her Chinese heritage on display. Her head hung down.

"You'll find someone. Apparently, it takes time and luck. Men don't come any better than Mac. When Mara found the courage to share her story with Mac, he tore down her walls bit by bit. He loves her despite all her imagined flaws. My biggest problem is I don't know what team to play for anymore. I'm exhausted from it all." She sighed heavily as her body sagged, willing the confusion to leave her body.

"What exactly happened between you and Sydney in the last couple of months?" Chloe's brows cinched with concern.

"When I returned from my vacation from hell, I broke up with Tom. He didn't seem too upset by the whole event. I got bored with his laid back style and non-existent personality. Our sex life played out like a 'How to' manual from steps one to three. Step one, kiss her. Step two, touch her. Step three, insert stick into hole. The predictability of it frustrated me and was totally unsatisfying." She shook her head. "I don't know why I stayed with him for so long." She sighed. "On the upside, he let me control and plan everything down to the last detail. He never challenged me." She hesitated and stared at Chloe. "You know me. I need a little friction. Someone who fires back." Boring seemed like death for her.

Tom was her second boyfriend. The thought of her first boyfriend left her with more questions than answers. Neither one of them sparked the fire she desired in her life. Sydney Polcheck lit her fire if only for a short time.

She met Chloe's gaze. "I found myself inexplicably drawn to Sydney." If she pursued her curiosity, she would have nothing to lose. "I had so many questions. What would it be like? Why was I so attracted to her? Was I a closet lesbian? I gave myself permission to be with her to try and find out the answers to my questions."

"Did you find what you were looking for?" Chloe said coyly.

"Apparently not." She rubbed her forehead. "Let's not dwell on what we don't have and tell me about our schedule today." She put an abrupt halt to discussing her love life, ignoring the pit sitting in her stomach.

She and Chloe went through the schedule for the day.

"What's this? Dragon Road Rides? I don't remember them as a client." She took notice of all the small details. Sometimes it was the larger picture that escaped her.

"They were the last minute addition you were supposed to meet with last night. They should be here any minute." Chloe fidgeted with the hem of her shirt.

"Who's 'they' exactly and why are you so nervous?" Anger surfaced with raw nerves.

"A model and a bike." Chloe's eyes locked with her.

"A model and a bicycle?" An interesting combination.

"A male model and a motorcycle." Chloe let out a breath and turned away, busying herself with something else on the desk. "I didn't set up for it because I wasn't sure how you wanted to shoot this. I know you like to talk to the client first before deciding on the shoot."

She eyed Chloe. Perhaps her nervousness had nothing to do with anything related to work. But she would get to the bottom of it.

CHAPTER 4

*D*ean *Wagner trudged* up Battery Place to his next assignment. He turned up his collar, shielding him from the cold wind whipping off the water snaking down the narrow alleys. As he rounded the corner to the back of the building, the delivery men were off loading the high-end bikes. He would play co-host while the photographer snapped away. He bristled at Mac's suggestion of babysitting some starter photographer whose apartment got tossed. Boo-hoo, poor baby.

He'd been read in on the case. The photographer wannabe needed protection from her ex-lover, a female operative. Sydney Polcheck, a CIA agent, had gone dark and disappeared. Their case involved Mara's late husband, Brock, who faked his death shortly after stealing millions from the Russians. When he reappeared in Mexico and kidnapped Mara, the Russians took care of him. Many questions went unanswered about the Russians' play in several illegal worldwide operations. Shadowing Mara's sister was the only possible way to get a lead in the case. Sometimes being in private security sucked, but he had no choice.

Mac went over the details and mentioned he thought Leigha experimented sexually and may not be a lesbian. It didn't matter. He wouldn't be interested. This wasn't real undercover work. But Mac convinced him the break-in was part of a bigger picture. He fumed over the fact his previous modeling experience, the curse, got him this assignment. Posing irritated him, but he had been told he was a natural.

He imagined her to be like many other female photographer he came across, plain and mousey. It might be a relief. His jaw locked as he gritted his teeth thinking of the high-maintenance women with their straightened hair, painted nails, collagen filled lips and Botox foreheads. They had a right to look their best, but the phony entitled attitude some of them had grated on his last friggin' nerve. The Devil had sent them all to this godforsaken city. He couldn't wait to go back to Australia, but his timeline stretched ahead of him with no end in sight.

He came to a stop, admiring the three polished artworks created by his good friend Keir O'Shea. The gas tank and back fender were done in flat black paint with an overspray of mica blue, apple red, and plume crazy purple flake. A chrome dragon stretching from front to back served as an accent. The combination of elements allowed each bike to project its own image. They garnered attention from people walking along the river who stopped to take notice of the unique designs. He would definitely be ordering one these babies soon.

His hands balled inside his jacket pockets. He breathed out through his nose as his hot breath clouded in the cold air. He took a moment to put on his professional face. There were worse gigs than this one. He let his fingers curl around the handlebars. They felt good in his hands. He leaned the bike away from him, nudging the kickstand up, and rolled the bike forward to the open freight elevator. Older buildings had freight elevators known for stalling out. That was fine by him. He might be able to escape for a while. It grinded its way up the shaft, struggling to continue upward. He lifted the grate and rolled the bike into the stark studio.

The clip sound of heels assaulted him. "Hi, you must be Dean Andersen. I'm Chloe. Thanks for bringing the bike up. You can set it up over there. We'll be with you in a moment." Her lips tweaked up as she winked at him.

He nodded, acknowledging his contact for this job. She was a short woman with black hair and big, black-rimmed glasses walking gracefully in her towering heels. Mac had to find an in because the photographer didn't want a detail.

She made her way across the studio to a woman looking down at her clipboard, concentrating on whatever kept her attention. His eyes lingered on her as curiosity bit him. He smirked. The photographer was exactly what he pictured, a mousey dreamer. Putty in his hands. His body relaxed at the notion he would have everything under control. He could be out of here sooner than expected. He bent over and put the kickstand in place, securing the bike.

Chloe glanced over her shoulder at him before she turned her attention to the blonde. She spoke to her in a low voice just out of earshot. Whatever she said didn't seem to move the listener. She finally tugged on her arm, moving her in his direction.

"Mr. Andersen, I'd like you to meet the photographer, Leigha Luccenzo. Leigha, this is Dean Andersen. He'll be modeling with the bikes from Dragon Road Rides."

He stood to his full height. She tilted her head back with a cool look in her eye as she sized him up. His guard went up. He took note of the beauty standing before him. She was a breath of fresh air from her glossy flaxen hair to her flawless skin. Her red wire glasses accented her hazel eyes. He held his breath in surprise. The encounter was unexpected.

She automatically extended her hand, unaffected by his presence. "Hi, nice to meet you. Please let us know if we can get you anything while you're here. I need a couple of minutes to set up for some initial shots and then we might decide to take the shoot outside." She pivoted on her heels as sharp clicks receded in the space.

His jaw flexed. She didn't even blink, completely disregarding him. Something unfamiliar flared in him. In that one moment she drew her line in the sand and it challenged him, stirring his senses. Things were about to get interesting.

He took in the sight of her. She hid under clothes that simply hung on her. Her outward appearance didn't match the woman she presented to him. She exuded strength and confidence. A wolf in shar-pei's clothing.

He always got his pick when it came to women. They easily submitted to his charms. But she barely acknowledged him. God knows he loved a good challenge. This golden lab needed a lesson in who was the pack leader. She wouldn't be controlling the show.

His eyes never left her as she worked around the bike setting lights, diffusers, and light meters. She operated with all the professionalism and knowledge of someone who knew her craft. He had a hard time keeping his eyes off of her, but he needed to stay focused. The assignment required him to gather intel and keep track of her.

He scanned the studio, taking note of its cleanliness, from the small kitchen to the floors and windows. Nothing out of place, a sure sign of OCD. The space showcased everything from exposed beams to spotless hardwood floors, yet she hid behind her monochrome pants suit, exposing nothing. Her dichotomy piqued his interest even more. She was hiding something. His eyes landed on the spotless shelf filled with pigs of all varieties except for one. Smashed to pieces, it lay in a careful pile at the end of the shelf. Why would anyone keep broken pieces? The homage to pigs seemed the total opposite to the gazelle of a woman in front of him.

He snapped out of his recon and caught her struggling to adjust a light high up. "Let me get that for you. Which way do you want it?" His voice softened.

"A little to the left." Her eyes stayed focused on the light.

"Do you need help with anything else? Do you want me to move the bike?" He invited her to look at him.

She denied his request when she simply said, "No, thank you," she answered him as if declining the offer of another piece of bread from a waiter.

"Chloe, would you be so kind as to get me a coffee down the street? I'm craving some caffeine." He laid his charm on thick, needing some alone time with the intriguing creature before him. All in the name of intel.

"We have coffee here if you want some." Chloe's head snapped up as uneasiness crossed her face.

"Would you be a love and please get me some Starbucks? It's the only coffee that agrees with my system." He emphasized it with a megawatt smile.

"It'll be fine. We have plenty of light. Go ahead and get him some coffee. There's nothing worse than a cranky model." Leigha smiled for the first time.

Oh, good. She was a smartass too.

Chloe grabbed her by the arm, moving her out of earshot. They huddled together. After Chloe whispered something in her ear, her body stiffened. Chloe looked over her shoulder and smiled while continuing to the door.

He smirked. "I see you're a seasoned professional when it comes to working with models."

"Yes, especially the diva variety." She turned and looked at him with hard eyes, her resting bitch face firmly in place.

He'd never met anyone so immune to his charm. "Oh, so you have already sized me up as a diva. It doesn't look like you and I are getting off to a very good start." He stepped closer into her personal space. "Truth, Dare or Care?"

She stood stick straight, meeting him face to face. Her ringless fingers curled around the edge of the clipboard. "What?"

"It's my game to get to know you. The responder gets to pick one."

"Care?" Her fingers curled tighter around the clipboard as sadness flashed across her eyes.

"I get to ask you about something you might have feelings for. You have to tell me the truth." He searched her face for anxiety but found none.

Without missing a beat she said, "Wouldn't that fall under Truth?"

"No. A truth can be lied about, but a care is written on your face." He reached out to touch a piece of hair that had fallen from her bun. She stepped away from him as expected. "The question is, are you game?"

"Truth." Her words held defiance.

"Why was Chloe so reluctant to leave you alone with me?" He stuffed his hands in his front pockets.

Her face went blank. "Well, aren't you observant? We're single women living in a big city. We have each other's backs so to speak."

"That makes sense and very smart." He liked the fact that she understood the dangers of the big city.

She gave him a small smile. Silence hung in the air as his eyes locked on hers.

"Aren't you going to ask me anything?" His chest tightened. There were so many questions he couldn't answer.

"No. I'm too busy taking care of those around me to play games, Mr. Andersen." She gave him a stand down soldier look. She would be calling the shots. "We have work to do and we're wasting precious light." Ending the conversation, she turned away, giving her full attention to her light meter.

"It's Dean. Mr. Andersen is my father."

Her head popped up and she turned back around.

"If we're going to be working together, you should probably call me Dean, Leigha."

She swallowed hard as if she were digesting the information. Nodding, a faint smile graced her lips as she turned to continue to work.

His eyes followed her, resigned to the tough uphill battle to convince her he was one of the good guys. She had her control in check, showing no fear or intimidation. Her demeanor said she either had a lot of experience as a photographer or a model, maybe both. But he had plenty himself. She proved to be a formidable opponent. He'd played this game before all too familiar with women who held secrets.

CHAPTER 5

Leigha was caught off guard, from the strength of his handshake to his ocean blue eyes. His mere presence confused and rattled her. She wasn't ready for someone like him. He challenged her. He seemed to read her words written in invisible ink. She had to be careful. He might start to read between the lines. The battle between them had begun. She needed to hold on.

Her attention turned to Chloe, who had returned, dragging her away from him. "Oh, my! He's beautiful with a capital B."

"Don't be fooled. He's probably gay. Most of them are." She acted unfazed by the encounter, wanting Chloe to buy her lie. Was the lie for her or Chloe?

"Oh, I don't think so. Not the way he looked at you. I think he stopped breathing." Chloe gave her half a smile and a wink as she crossed her arms over her chest.

Looking over her shoulder in Dean's direction, Chloe sighed. "Regardless, this is going to be a great shoot. Good luck. I'll go check the light outside." She walked past her and hurried out the door.

Alone in the studio, she could feel his gaze sear her back. Goosebumps formed on her arms from the mixture of attraction and fear, or was it fear of attraction? She struggled to focus as her emotions roared to life.

"So you have quite the studio here. How long have you been a professional photographer?" His words traveled on a British accent gone wild straight from the outback. He came up close behind her. His warm breath wisped across her cheek.

"Long enough to know what I'm doing, if that's your question," she bristled.

He responded with a questioning hum.

Her eyes remained on the equipment as she managed to avoid looking at him. She worked with mostly female models over the years. This was her first opportunity to work with a male model in a long time. He unnerved her, but she didn't know why. Her body lacked flexibility moving with calculated effort. The heat of his eyes tried to penetrate her. Sex appeal rolled off him in waves bombarding her senses.

"So how can I help?"

When she turned around the top of her head almost slammed into his chin. Startled, she stumbled backward as he caught her arm. After she steadied herself, she jerked her arm away. Her breath quickened.

He let go immediately. "I'm sorry. I didn't want you to fall." Sorrow filled his eyes. She didn't quite understand where it came from.

"It's okay. I'm not used to people in my personal

space." She abruptly turned to refocus on her work instead of how his touch warmed her cold spots.

She turned to face him with hands on her hips. "Truth."

"Ah. Someone has caught onto my game." He smiled like a kid who shared the secret password to the clubhouse.

"How did you end up with this gig?"

His tone softened at her question as his smile fell. "Keir is one of my best mates. He started building his dream bikes, fueled by his passion and vision. His bikes are one-offs. Each bike's front fender is designed to look like a dragon's head as the body makes its way into a tail at the back fender." His hand followed the lines of the bike and his eyes lit up from the inside as he described the passion he and his friend had for bikes.

He peeled off his shirt, exposing a dragon tattoo. Her heart beat in her chest as she stopped herself from moving forward, wanting to reach out and touch him.

"What do you think?" His smile brightened his eyes.

The dragon's head started on his left shoulder, winding around his bicep, and the tail ended at his elbow. He flexed his bicep, making the dragon move. Her mouth went dry. For as many male models as she had been around in her life, he won the prize for perfection. Broad, round shoulders, cut abs, and an ass that filled out his jeans, highlighted his lithe body. She wanted to take him in all at once but wasn't sure where to start. She needed to rein it in.

"I think you're...it's beautiful. Why black and

red?" Her fingers itched to skim his fire to melt her ice.

"The last time I saw him, we decided to celebrate Keir's first sale with a dragon tattoo. We designed a black dragon with red flames arcing over its head. It trails down its back as the tail turned into another flame. Keir picked the black for its association with the Chinese 'Dark Warrior.' He worked as a US Navy SEAL in Afghanistan. After several tours, he came back to the States half the man he left as, with a missing arm and leg. IEDs are unforgiving, but he's the kind of man that nothing holds him back. I picked the red for its aboriginal meaning of protection." His eyes darkened. He gave her a glimpse of the secrets he kept locked down.

Her heart ached for Keir's story. She would make sure the photos were the best she ever shot. She didn't want to dwell on the pain of his story. "Your dragon has some interesting history." She left it open for him to continue. Her eyes met his as the darkness left.

He stared at her with intensity without taking the bait. "I think the shot would be best taken showing the dragon. Don't you?"

"Care."

"I think you might be using this game to your advantage." He smirked.

"Where did you go just now?" Her hands gripped her pants, preventing them from reaching out to comfort him. She wasn't sure what had gotten into her.

His face fell and pain skated across his eyes. "There are a lot of things I can't talk about. War is an ugly, unforgiving beast."

"I'm sorry." Her words floated on a whisper. She let out a sigh. "I need to set the lighting and angle it."

He brushed by her to put his shirt down. She couldn't help but stare at the dragon on his shoulder. He let out a heavy sigh through his nose, as his heated breath crossed her forehead. Her fingers drummed on her thigh, wanting to feel the heat of his blood beneath the ink.

Chloe burst into the studio from the stairwell. She jumped back from him like a teenage caught stealing a kiss from a boy.

"I tried to get back as soon as possible. I know how the boss lady can be." Chloe's eyes roamed his body from head to toe.

The bing went off in Leigha's head like a cell phone with a text. She rolled her eyes at Chloe's perusal of his physique.

He took a sip of his coffee. "Chloe, I can't thank you enough for the coffee. We divas can be so demanding." He winked.

"No problem." Chloe sighed.

Leigha had stepped back from the scene with hands on her hips. He turned in her direction with a glint in his eyes as he drank the coffee. She hadn't intended for him to see that side of her. She turned around to tend to the bike.

Chloe followed behind her. "What do you need me to do?"

"Nothing." She words were curt. She put the back of her hand to her forehead as she leaned on the leather bike seat. "I'm sorry. That came out harsher than I wanted it to. It's been a rough couple of days."

Chloe backed away. "I have other things I can be doing. I'll leave you to your work."

"Are you okay?" He moved closer to her but outside the perimeter of her personal space. Her body sagged over the bike seat leaning on her hands.

"I'll be all right. My apartment got broken into the other night. From what I can tell, nothing was taken, which means they didn't find what they were looking for," she blurted out, biting her lower lip to keep from telling him more.

"Maybe you should have someone stay with you, like Chloe." His concern for her flared inside her.

She shot upright and turned to him, brushing off the suggestion. "No, I'll be fine. Time heals all wounds, right?" Her arms wrapped around her as she gave him her fake smile. He bent his head sideways as if examining her.

"Yes, and we all have wounds, don't we?" His eyes penetrated hers in a stare off. "Let's start shooting, shall we?" He put his coffee down and stood next to the bike.

She snapped her shield back in place, ready for the day ahead.

"You don't mind if I play music, do you?" He wore that damn smirk again.

"No, go right ahead," she replied, curious about his taste in music.

He played the first song, "Sex Is Good" by Saving Abel and laughed with a low rumble.

For next couple of hours, he took directions from her effortlessly. Keeping her distance, she stood hunched over her medium format camera. She gave orders but took few of his suggestions. A low grumble could be heard when she didn't accept his advice on a shot. The flow happened naturally between them, but she never touched him. A rule was a rule. You never touch the model. But she was like a cat in heat. Her skin itched to rub up against him. Maybe he could be her boy toy. She didn't need the next big relationship. She needed a distraction.

His playlist ended as his word cut the air. "Truth."

"Maybe," she said coyly.

"You look like the cat that ate the canary. What's the smile about?" He closed in, trying to read her.

"Nothing. We're running out of natural light. I think we need to call it a day. You're a natural in front of the camera. How long have you been modeling?" Her body relaxed, leaving behind the precision.

"Long enough, I suppose. You're excellent at giving directions. Can I look at what you shot so far?"

He stood over six foot with dark blond hair and sun-kissed ends. His blue eyes had a range of emotions. He was a photographer's dream.

He came over to stand next to her and rubbed up against her shoulder. She backed away, feeling his fire.

"These are fantastic. Your use of shadow and light is amazing. Keir is going to be pumped about these."

She gazed up at him as a wisp of golden hair fell from her tight bun, tickling her nose. He reached up, tucking it behind her ear. His finger caressed her cheek as he let it fall. His touch mad her shiver and she took a step backward. Needles stabbed at her chest as if they remembered something, throwing her off balance.

"I hope he's happy with them. I need to wrap up. You can let yourself out when you're ready. Oh, and take one of my cards in case you need me. I'll see you tomorrow." She turned away briskly, ignoring the energy between them. She didn't want her lines blurred.

CHAPTER 6

"*See you tomorrow.*" Dean's words evaporated in the air. He stood with his shirt hanging in his hands, confused by his encounter with her. Her reference to healing wounds stabbed him, hitting too close to home. Her eyes and body language spoke of an untold story. She kept a tight rein on her emotions, holding her wounds close. He wanted to know about her wounds and where they came from. His insatiable need to know who she was behind the façade ate at him.

When he was read in on the case, he found out her apartment had been broken into, but that didn't account for her conflicting messages. Something else was at work. She struggled with something. The closer he got to her the more he wanted to find out what made her tick. His head spun. The cure was a long ride on a bike that gave him an adrenaline rush.

As he came out of the door onto the street, the hair on the back of his neck stood on end. Across the street from the studio sat two top of the line Range Rovers, one in gray and the other in deep blue, both with blackout windows.

He made his way to his red Ducati 959 Panigale, never giving away his awareness of the vehicles. He put on his helmet and started the engine. At the same time, the blue Range Rover's engine turned over. The drivers were at the start line.

He pulled into slow moving traffic, baiting the Range Rover. When he was sure of his tail, he opened up the Ducati. The bike ate up the road with speed and maneuvered through any obstacle.

Racing at high speed was second nature to him. He spent his youth on a bike track. They had no idea who they were messin' with. The light traffic allowed him to tear through the streets, weaving his way around cars. His strategy would lead them away from New York City and into New Jersey. Power pumped through his veins. This was what he lived for, the chase. But it was hard to tell who was the cat and who was the mouse. As soon as they hit the city limits, he slowed down, shortening the distance between them. He wanted to get a closer look at the amateurs.

They beat him to it. The shot sounded before the bullet whizzed by his shoulder. Game time. These guys wanted a piece of him. The Ducati hadn't even hit its peak yet as he revved it into top gear. He left the Range Rover in the dust as they shot wildly from the window.

He wove around the quiet streets of Jersey to make sure he lost them. When he confirmed it was clear, he made his way back to his apartment on the Upper East Side. His thoughts churned, trying to figure out their angle. Were they trying to scare him? Did this have something to do with the case? God knows he had enough enemies, so the possibilities were endless. He parked the bike in the underground parking, tucking it away from interested onlookers.

He removed his helmet as the sweat poured off his forehead. His heart pounded in his chest. He craved the rush. It gave him a release from his pent-up energy. Leigha pushed all the buttons he had ignored for years. He didn't want to feel or be curious. His insulated world gave him comfort without complications.

He made his way up to his luxury penthouse he had inherited from his grandmother, a world-famous opera singer. His thoughts traveled back to Leigha. They were somewhat alike. His grandmother wore her costumes like armor for entertainment. Leigha bolted her armor to her for cover. He wanted to know the woman behind the drab exterior. It wouldn't be easy, but if he ever caught her with her guard down, he would find a way in.

He threw his helmet on the plastic-covered couch and it stuck to it like rubber cement. God, he really needed to remodel the place. The entire place reeked of vintage funky old people smell. The only places that reflected him were the bedroom, den, and kitchen. It looked as if two different people lived there. He couldn't even bring women back to his place.

He took a quick shower before getting into bed then dialed Leigha's number.

"Hello?" She answered after the third ring.

"Hey, I just wanted to make sure you got home okay today." He tried to sound casual as if he hadn't been chased down by gun-toting maniacs.

"Who is this?" Her voice laced with fear.

"It's Dean. Are you okay?" Curiosity nipped at him as to why she was so spooked.

"Yeah. Why are you calling me to see if I'm okay?" She didn't miss a beat. Perceptive and beautiful made for a deadly combination.

"I noticed a pair of Range Rovers parked across the street when I left. It made me a little uneasy." He rolled his eyes at his choice of words. He couldn't remember the last time he felt uneasy about anything. He had been trained to handle these situations without nerves.

"Why would you notice a Range Rover parked across the street?" Her question was laced with suspicion.

"It had dark windows and didn't look right, that's all," he shot back a little too hard. She had a keen sense and he needed to watch himself.

"Thank you for checking on me. I'm home safe and sound. I've got to go." She clicked off before he had a chance to say goodbye.

He had every intention of getting himself off with thoughts of her, but not after that exchange. She left herself out of reach. He couldn't get a steady read on her. Her mysterious ways made him a moth to her flame.

He called Mac next, needing to get his input on the latest development.

"What's up?" Mac answered the phone, trying to control his panting.

"Oh, am I interrupting something?" He laughed at his timing.

"Aye, and she can't wait, so get to it." Everyone knew Mara came above all else and probably many times.

"I had a tail when I left the studio today. One Range Rover took the bait while the other one stayed behind. They took stray shots like they wanted to scare me but not kill me. Any thoughts?"

"Yeah, I have a thought. Where the fuck is Leigha?" He had never heard Mac yell before, but a lion's roar paled in comparison.

"Jesus, calm the fuck down already. I called her and she's fine. I believe she used the words safe and sound, so don't get your panties in a bunch, mate." He hated being called out.

"If I weren't buck naked, I would come over there and pull your head out of your arse. You're supposed to be protecting her at all times. Consider this your one free pass. There won't be another one. Did you get a license plate number?"

"No, I was being chased, remember? I think this is bigger than we originally thought. If you're going to shoot at me, why not take me out?" This case might prove to be more interesting than he thought.

"Good question. I'll look into it. These guys are professionals. They have her covered. In the meantime, find a way to stay closer to Leigha. If one hair on her head is hurt, I'll never hear the end of it." Mac hung up before Dean could give him one of his smart-mouthed retorts.

He failed to mention this scare tactic might be one of his enemies catching up with him. But something told him probably not. This puzzle had missing pieces.

CHAPTER 7

After a night of tossing and turning, Leigha cursed her subconscious. She thought the transition to sleeping in her apartment would be easy. But her nightmare returned in full technicolor. Her dreams possessed more strength each time, giving her one more clue. In this dream she heard Benjamin, her first boyfriend's voice, as she fought against something or someone. She woke up in terror, becoming more frustrated at not being able to see the whole picture. Fear tightened around her. She couldn't shake the feeling she had hurt someone. Was she really capable of that?

She shuffled to her dresser and looked in the mirror. Her reflection revealed bags under eyes, sallow skin, tight dry lips, and a tumbleweed on her head. She needed to find out what her nightmares were about before they swallowed her whole. Her hands shook at the prospect of living like this for the rest of her life. Tears shined in her eyes. She wiped them away. No. Hell no. She would fight through this. Her nightmare may reveal something terrible about her, but she couldn't go on like this. *Stay with your routine.*

She went for her usual run to clear her head and got to the studio early. The peace and quiet of her sanctuary grounded her while she sipped white tea. The overcast day added to her somber mood. She stood in her regular spot by the window, peering down on the Hudson.

The grinding of the freight elevator broke the silence, catching her attention. Too early for Chloe to be making an appearance, her heart raced. She grabbed her umbrella as a weapon. She held her breath and waited anxiously to see who stepped off the elevator. Gripping the umbrella handle tighter, her heartbeat kicked up. She had taken Mac's warning seriously, but then got a strange call from Dean last night. What was that about anyway?

The grate opened and Dean stepped out, striding across the studio. His presence moved the air as a calm came over her. He was goddamn gorgeous. But there was something else about him that moved her. She couldn't quite put her finger on the attraction. There was more to him than his looks. She couldn't ignore him, no matter how hard she tried. Her eyes followed him before he saw her. He owned the space as any model worth their salt would. He seemed at home in a studio in front of lights and cameras. The strum in her chest caught her off guard. When he finally spotted her, his eyes were devoid of emotion until he stood in front of her. She must have looked like a deer in headlights.

"Are you okay? You look scared shitless." His brows pinched together as he squared his shoulders, with hands on his hips. He reached for her umbrella. "I don't think you would have done any damage with this."

"No, probably not. I'm fine. I wasn't expecting you this early. Chloe's usually the one in after me." She fumbled through her words.

"Why do you always say you're fine when you're clearly not?" Irritation etched his voice.

"What else am I supposed to do, fall apart?" she said defensively.

"Yes. Sometimes falling apart is okay." Hurt covered his face.

"Falling apart isn't an option for me." She yearned to lean on him.

His eyes tightened and the muscles in his jaw flexed. He stared at her through questioning eyes. She couldn't decipher his reaction.

"Yeah, well, I want this over with. I've got better things to do," he said tersely.

His words slapped her. She recognized his coolness. His disregard of her reminded her of her father's dismissal. She had learned to reject others before they rejected her. But she didn't want to reject him. He touched something inside her.

The teacup trembled slightly in her hands. Regret bubbled to the surface as tears glassed her eyes. "Care," she whispered. "I'm sorry. You called last night to check if I was okay and I was totally rude to you. The last couple of days have been rough for me. But it's no excuse." She hung her head, peering into her cup of nothing.

His hands wrapped around hers on the cup. "Do you want to talk about it?" His kind words were a relief.

The tension left her body as the warmth of his

hands softened her and stopped the trembling. "No. Not right now."

"Leigha, under that tough exterior, you have a lot going on. I'm here if you want to talk. Sometimes it's easier to talk to a stranger and then the stranger becomes a friend." He smiled.

She managed to pull back her tears as her eyes met his. His sincerity was refreshing. But she needed to hide the sharp pieces of her nightmare. "I want to take the bikes outside today."

He finished her thought, "The overcast day makes for great photography." He had a warm, genuine smile as he released his hands from hers.

"Can I offer you some coffee? I'll warn you now, I don't have Starbucks." She laughed, lightening the mood between them.

"Well, I don't know what I'm going to do then. We divas have demands that need to be met." He bit his lower lip as he tried to stay serious.

"They can make all the demands they want, but they probably won't be fulfilled."

"I think I'd like to fulfill your demands." His confidence took center stage.

The air hummed between them as heat rose to her cheeks, making her blush under his gaze. Ignoring his comment, she pushed off the window frame with her hip.

"Let's get this rolling before the sun comes out and wrecks everything." She enjoyed his sense of humor and banter. He blurred her edges, ruffling her resolve to stay in control at all times. But she couldn't let him in. It required her to lower her shield. She didn't do that for just anyone. She wasn't sure she had ever let anyone in.

The elevator grinded again. Chloe came clicking across the floor, beaming from ear to ear. All her sunshine was aimed at Dean.

"Good morning, everyone." She bubbled.

He smiled at Chloe and returned her greeting. His gaze swung back in her direction.

She knew who Chloe dreamed about last night. Her back got up. Jealousy was a foreign concept. She tapped it down, staying focused on the job at hand.

He took the bikes down the elevator and behind the building, placing them in front of the river. The setting was ideal. A heavy black iron railing behind the bikes served as an accent with the riverfront buildings across the water. The buildings ranged from modern to turn of the century, helping convey the message these bikes were made for anyone.

Dressed in motorcycle boots, jeans, T-shirt, and a black leather jacket, he made the scene come together. While Chloe fussed with diffusers and lights, she took some preliminary shots of the bikes with the backdrop.

Her head lifted as the heavy bass of Ginuwine's song "Pony" blared through a small amplifier.

"What? I need to get in the mood." He flashed her a smile at the implications of the song.

His boldness drew her to him. With every shot, his clear blue eyes pierced straight through her. She couldn't deny he made her nervous, but she couldn't pinpoint why. He poked at parts of her she didn't want poked. There were so many sides to him, from dominant, warm, and funny. As she bent over her camera, she shifted from one foot to the other, trying to ease her nervous energy. He had soul and sex appeal. Her attraction to him irritated her. This wasn't what she needed in her life. It would end in another disappointment. Besides, he couldn't possibly want her.

His playlist continued with songs from Keith Sweat like "Nobody" and "I Want Her." She remembered Raquelle's comment that Keith Sweat's songs made babies. Babies? They had never crossed her mind.

"Look, I need you to turn away from the right side. I don't like how the shadow plays on your face." Her photographer eye knew exactly what to look for in the shot.

He retorted, "I think I know my body well enough to know what shadows look good on me. Besides, I think a little shadow would be good. It'll add mystery, like the bike."

"Hey, who's the photographer and who's the model?" She raised her voice as her nerves came undone.

He swung his leg over the bike. His long strides ate the space between them, meeting her face to face. "I know you're a control freak and all, but we have to work together to get through this. I've been in this business long enough to know what works and what doesn't. I know my body. I'm not just a handsome face, Leigha." His hands fell from his hips and his eyes pleaded with her to give him some slack.

The way he said her name made her weak in the knees. The air intensified between them as they battled for control. He didn't back down from her. She had always gotten her way, having people acquiesce to her especially during a shoot. The power and heat radiating off of him coated her skin with lust. He flustered her. The strike to her match.

"Fine. Let's get this done." She swallowed the lump in her throat as she skimmed her hand over the top of her head. Getting rid of him would be in her best interest.

He stood there for a moment, penetrating her with his eyes as they flickered with wonder. They scanned her face as if memorizing it.

Stalking back to the bike, he sat down firmly. "Let's do this." His features softened as he got back into model mode.

She breathed a shallow sigh of relief, unsure of what she really wanted from him.

As the day wore on, they started to attract a crowd as the street became busy. Women were interested in him while the men were interested in the bikes. The ladies got a show they would never forget as he preened like a peacock. He peeled his T-shirt off, revealing a black wife beater and his glorious tattoos.

A beautiful blond woman approached him from the crowd and gave him her number. Without even a glance, he stuffed the paper in his back pocket as he looked at Leigha with a smirk, covering his eyes with Aviators.

She kept her resting bitch face in check, not giving him an ounce of emotion. She wouldn't be revealing anything to him.

The shadows of late afternoon approached as Chloe busied herself packing up the equipment. She had shot the pictures she needed for the day.

For some inexplicable reason, she was emotionally spent. Photographing him did things to her she couldn't explain, making her antsy. She usually didn't take a run at night, but this might be a first, running as far away from him as she could get. They worked as a team, hauling everything back up to the studio.

Chloe left for the day, leaving the two of them alone in the studio. The sun managed to break out in streams from the clouds, giving the studio a wash of cool color.

"How did the shoot go today? Can I see what you did?" He stood next to her, taking up her share of oxygen. Her racing heart betrayed her need to stay within her constraints.

She scanned through the photos, standing next to him. His breath ruffled her hair. The thrum in her chest came back stronger this time. It tilted her. She needed something to hold on to, preferably him.

"You have quite the eye. I can understand why you were picked for the job." His compliment shouldn't have mattered to her, but it did. Compliments were far and few between. After his raging bull performance, his tone had softened and fell over her like a favorite blanket. She appreciated his interest in her work and getting the right shot.

"Thank you. You're easy to work with. Well, I should say you became easier to work with as the day went on. You really understand your face and body as well as what angles work best for you and the bike." Her voice hitched on the last syllable, giving away her admiration of him.

"Truth. How long did you model for?" He continued to look at the LCD screen of her camera.

No one outside of the business could understand how you have to look at yourself from the outside. A model must have an almost unnatural yet intimate knowledge of every part of their body. The most minute shift could change the whole effect of the shot.

Ice ran in her veins, shutting him out. She didn't want to revisit her past. Her body straightened like an arrow. "It was a while ago. Not worth getting into. I guess we should call it a night." She pulled her camera from him and turned to put it away, giving him her back.

"I'm sorry. I didn't mean to intrude." He gently took her arm to turn her around to look at him. His hand slid down her arm to hold her hand.

On some level she appreciated he didn't let her off the hook. Her past pushed its way to the front. "It wasn't a great time in my life. When you're young, things can get confusing. You start to trust a little too much. As you know, it's a world onto itself full of illusions and manipulations."

His smile said he understood. She wanted to swim in the depths of his eyes. A peace came over her she had never experienced. But wasn't sure she'd be able to trust it.

He pushed a stray hair out of her eyes. "Have you ever been on a bike before? It's the best feeling in the world. Total freedom. How about we go for a ride? We can take one from the Dragon Road Rides collection." He sounded like a teenage boy trying to convince his girlfriend.

Her flight or fight reaction kicked in. She needed to shut this down. He was getting too close and too comfortable. "I'll take a pass. I'm wiped. Maybe some other time." She couldn't find her bearings when it came to him. One minute she basked in his oversexed heat and the next he said or did something to make her shut down. Her emotions ran all over the place.

"I'll let myself out then. I'm going to take one of the bikes from the garage. Today was good, Leigha. You do great work and have quite an eye. Keir is going to be stoked. I'll see you tomorrow." Sadness draped over his face as his eyes searched hers for answers. He grabbed his jacket and headed for the door.

The minute her name left his lips, something exploded in her. She reveled in the way it flowed off his tongue as if she already belonged to him. As much as she liked the view of his back end, she didn't like the feel of him leaving. God, what was going on with her?

She gathered her things and headed down to the lobby. As she approached the doors to the street, she stopped cold in her tracks. Parked directly across the street was a blue Range Rover with tinted windows. Chills skidded across her skin.

CHAPTER 8

Leigha's gut reaction told her to call the number saved from the previous night.

His voice washed over her with comfort. "Leigha?"

"Hi, you know that ride you wanted to take? Now would be a good time." Her voice trembled, skipping over the words.

"What's going on?" Urgency spiked in his voice.

"There's a Range Rover parked across the street and I have a bad feeling. Can you come and get me, please?" She wasn't used to begging.

"Listen to me. I'm going to come out of the garage and hand you a helmet. Yes, you have to wear one. Jump on the back and hold on tight. Do you understand?" The authority in his voice left no room for negotiation.

"Yes." The situation had become sever.

"Good. I'm on my way."

She stood far enough away from the tinted glass doors not to be seen from the road. Slinging her purse across her body, she dumped in her phone and camera, getting ready to run. The rumble from the bike shook the glass doors. His face was surrounded a black helmet with silver stripes with the visor up. He came to a screeching halt on the Red Dragon bike. She ran to him, grabbed the helmet, and placed it on her head. Her bun took up the extra space, giving her a snug fit. The Range Rover, facing in the opposite direction, started up its engine.

They roared off down the street. Having never been on a bike before, she held on for dear life. Her long legs molded to the back of his. She gripped his waist and tucked her head behind his shoulder blades.

The Range Rover turned to follow them but halfway down the street came to an abrupt stop.

She turned her head and yelled up into his ear, "They've stopped. They're not following us."

He nodded his head to acknowledge he heard her. Turning his head slightly, he said, "You're mine now. Sit tight. We're going for a ride."

She had no choice, trapped with nowhere to go. She was way out of her element. Anxiety should have taken over, but instead calm drifted over her. He took the reins from her once again, pushing her boundaries. Her heart lightened. The heaviness of her shield had been lifted from her, for the moment. He had the control. She was helpless to do anything about it. Worse yet, she barely knew him.

She could tell they were headed out of the city and into New Jersey. As she relaxed, her grip loosened from around his waist. The air twisted around her arms and legs as the bike rumbled underneath her. Thrusting forward at a high rate of speed they seemed to fly above the ground. Her hands clutched his leather jacket. He wrapped his fingers around her hands, smoothing over the knuckles. Gentleness came through the rough pads of his fingertips. They sent the message, 'Stay calm. I've got this.'

After about an hour of driving, he turned off the highway and headed toward the shoreline. As they got closer, the ocean breeze picked up, caressing them. She sniffed the fresh ocean air, still warm from the summer with a hint of autumn.

He rolled the bike to a stop near the boardwalk. During the summer Asbury Park drew crowds from all over the world as people walked the famous boardwalk and visited the theatre. The cool breezes of autumn held less appeal for visitors to come to the beach. The vacant buildings made it a ghost town filled with her childhood memories. She and her sisters would run in and out of the small stores, get scolded and then beg for ice cream, getting their way every time. The memories warmed her heart.

He got off the bike then gently lifted the helmet from her head. Her bun began to fall apart. She reached to secure the wild hairs back into her bun. He grabbed her hands. Without a word he placed her hands in her lap. He took out each hairpin, letting her hair fall as the breeze ruffled it. His tenderness held more intimacy than it should have.

"I think I would like to see you a little less uptight. Your hair is beautiful. Leave it down. Please." His eyes were soft and sincere.

"I'm not uptight. It's a neater look for work," she said in a weak defense, put off by his words.

He smirked, taking her hand as she swung her leg over the bike to stand up.

"Let's walk." He laced his fingers in hers with a familiarity of having done it a million times before. Comfort started to form between them.

Her instinct was to resist, but she gave into the relief of having him take over. The wind tangled her hair around her head like a turban. She closed her other hand into a fist, fighting the urge to tie her hair back to keep it out of her eyes. For the first time in a long time the tension that wrapped up her body slid away. He took it from her. Out here she didn't have any decisions to make, people to worry about or clients to satisfy. He plucked her away from all of it.

He came to a halt at the top of the stairs that led to the beach. He released her hand, took off his boots, and peeled off his socks. Tilting his head sideways from below, he said, "What are you waiting for? Strip off those shoes so you can feel the sand between your toes."

Like a puppet on the end of a string, she took off her shoes. She loved the feel of cool sand under her feet. A smug smile crossed his face knowing he had won a small battle. He rolled up his pants, stuffed his socks in his boots, and carried them down the stairs.

"Come on, Princess Leigha." His words floated away on the soft breeze, chased by his laugh.

"I'm not the princess. That belongs to my sister Raquelle." Her words were indignant.

He laughed louder. "No. I don't imagine you are. A princess would let other people take care of things. You take care of everything all the time."

She stared at him crossing her arms in front of her. His observations infuriated her mostly because he was right. "I don't think this is a good idea. You can take me home now." She turned and started for the stairs.

He dropped his boots and turned her to face him. With hands on his hips, determination was set in his eyes. "Oh, that is a great idea. I could take you home. But I'm not going to. I brought you out here to relax. You're like watching an emotional rollercoaster. You need to let loose a little. Truth." He paused. "What's with the Range Rovers? Ex-boyfriend?" Acting was part of the job.

She turned back and let her arms fall in a huff, letting go of her shoes. He cornered her, forcing her into a place she didn't want to go.

"I honestly don't know. And that would be ex-girlfriend."

"Even better. I like threesomes." He wiggled his brows.

"Oh, I bet you do." She picked up a shoe and threw it at him. He ducked and laughed. "It may have something to do with the break-in. At every turn there's something else to put me on edge." Tears welled up, but she wouldn't let them fall.

A few small steps put him inches from her. "Come sit with me in the sand. Please?" He said it on a plea as if he needed something from her.

"The fact that I'm a lesbian doesn't deter you?" She wanted to know what he thought about her proclamation.

"Nah. I like a good challenge. Are you sure you're a lesbian?"

"I'm not sure what I am." She swallowed down her doubt.

He held her by the elbow, guiding them closer to the water's edge. She sat next to him in comfortable silence. A nurturing man hid beneath a tough exterior. He tried to give her something she didn't even know she needed. Peace of mind. He called her out on it. Her emotions skated around wary of the holes she could fall through on this piece of thin ice. She looked over at him as longing veiled his face.

"What's wrong?" She turned her body to face him, interested in his soft underbelly.

He stared out at the horizon searching for something. "The beach always reminds me of home. I grew up on the beaches in Australia. They bring a sense of peace and longing." His voice tightened with restrained emotions.

"Are you going back soon?" Her fingers yearned to reach out and touch his soft spot in hopes it would rub off on her.

"No. Can't. Not yet." He bristled. His jaw tightened. "We're not here to talk about me. We're here to unravel you a bit."

"So a handsome model brings me to the beach to unravel me and what, jump my bones?" Her counter held bitterness and a warning.

He turned to her, resting his elbow on his bent knee. "Spoken like a model who's had her share of being hit on. Let me tell you what I know. Your emotions are all over the place. One minute you're soft, the next cold as ice. You crave the friction of being challenged because not many people challenge you. Oh, and now might be a good time for me to tell you I love a good challenge. You are smart, beautiful, and I think you might have a sense of humor under all your fierceness." His blue eyes sparkled diving into her soul.

She faced the ocean, hugging her knees to her chest. Her transparency shook her, stunned by how easily he read her. Without looking at him, she said, "I have a lot going on right now. It's been one thing after another. I don't know which way to turn anymore. And now might be a good time for me to mention that you're a pompous ass, sometimes." She wouldn't let him off the hook. Who did he think he was, Freud?

"Touché. You might say observing people is a hobby of mine. Watching people helps keep me aware of those who might have wandering hands during a shoot."

Her head came up and turned to him. "I never thought about men getting molested. I always assumed it only happened to women models. My memories from long ago still haunt me." Blowing out a breath, a tight string let go a bit to give her some wiggle room in the confines of her web. She rubbed the side of her neck with her hand.

"What haunts you?" He pushed a few strands of hair behind her ear, letting the tops of his fingers and thumb skim her cheek.

Her fingers curled painfully into her neck. She fought with the idea of revealing her nightmare to him. Tears pushed their way to her eyes of their own accord. Someone showing interest in her threw her off-kilter.

He leaned over and murmured, "Secrets have a way of destroying people from the inside out.

Yours are eating away at you." He took her chin in his fingers and turned her face to him. "Your secret's safe with me. We all have them. Maybe one day, I'll make you the keeper of mine."

Being the keeper of someone's secret was a valuable gift. She wanted to take a leap of faith with him. He already saw through her, leaving little to hide.

"While I was on vacation in Cancun, my sister Mara got kidnapped by her dead husband." She waited for his reaction but found none.

"Go on." He looked pensive.

"She had been abused by him during their marriage. That's when my nightmares returned in full force."

Sympathy softened his features. "I know something about nightmares. Can you tell me more?" He caressed her cheek.

"I can't. They come in fragments. I wake up frustrated, not knowing what they are about. I feel like if I could open that door it might change my life." Tears trailed down her cheeks. He wiped them away with his thumb. When she realized she was crying in front of him, she jerked back.

Curiosity flared in his eyes at her reaction. "Maybe you need to let go of your need to control everything. Give it to someone else. You're going to implode one day. Letting go might open that door." The truth of his words penetrated her.

She laughed. "Yeah. Easier said than done." Her shoulders sagged with exhaustion.

"How about if I get you home? We can talk more tomorrow." He stood, offering his hands as help.

She took his hands and stood up, gazing into eyes that held their own secrets. The soft silken cord bound them closer.

"Wait. I want to take your picture. You are so at home at the beach." She grabbed the camera from her bag and took several shots of him looking out to sea. As he looked back at the lens, his face held peace, sadness, and hope. She captured all three. His eyes were the frosted glass for his ghosts.

She lowered her camera. "Why can't you go back to Australia?" Something hitched in her chest. She wasn't sure she wanted to know the answer.

"Because that's where my nightmare lives." He turned his head away from her.

She put her camera away and held out her hand. "Seems like we both know something about nightmares. Not exactly a good thing to have in common."

He kissed her forehead as they walked back to the bike. His kiss was pure tenderness. The sound of the ocean faded behind it.

The ride back to the city left her contemplative. She let what happen between them sink in. He wasn't afraid to challenge her, making her confront her nightmares. But he also offered comfort and strength. Without knowing it, he let her peek behind his curtain.

He pulled up to the curb and she took off her helmet.

"Would you mind walking me up?"

"Sure," he responded without emotion.

They walked in silence down the hall to her apartment door. Brittle tension hung in the air. He seemed detached, as if something had triggered in him. Something had pushed him away from her.

"Are you okay?" she asked quietly.

"Yea, it's been a long day. I almost became the keeper of a secret. I hope I can help you untangle it." He smiled at his choice of words. Leaning over, he kissed her cheek. His kiss warmed her skin but held no fire, just understanding. "I'll see you tomorrow, Leigha." He walked away. Something twisted in her heart. His secrets ran deep. She doubted any of them had a keeper.

CHAPTER 9

Dean needed to wrap up this shoot sooner rather than later. She was starting to wade in. Soon she would be diving beneath his surface. Her many facets were too much of a draw, each one more fascinating than the last. For some unknown reason, she brought out the protector in him. He wanted to hold her to him, keeping her safe from her nightmare. He was sure it held the answers to all her control issues. Resisting the urge to get closer required him to let go of that side of himself.

Getting closer meant she would start to see through him. His secrets stayed buried under lock and key. He made sure of that. Talking about them made him itch. He slept like a trained Special Op with one eye open at all times. His bed resembled a tornado most mornings after he thrashed around trying to beat away the ghosts of his past.

She always came back to him in murky dreams, taking his ability to breathe from him. The one woman he failed to keep safe. The one woman he needed to protect from her monster. Her death squeezed his chest, begging for release. Shooting at the range got rid of some of the anger. He made her monster the target over and over again. But that son of a bitch was still alive. She was dead.

He watched his phone dance across the table, vibrating with a call. "Yea."

"Well, good morning to you, sunshine." He could almost see Mac smiling on the other side of the phone.

"What's up, mate?"

"We tracked those Range Rovers through the CCTV and found the plate numbers. They led us back to the Russian consulate. We thought we were just dealing with the Russian mob, but it looks like we have the government involved too. What I can't figure out is why they are going after Leigha." The receiver picked up his heavy sigh.

"Christ. They followed us last night but stopped halfway down the street. What the hell for? What the fuck do they want?" His nerves amped up with the thought of having anything Russian following Leigha.

"I don't know, but I need you on her like superglue. And let me be clear, I didn't say 'in her,' I said 'on her.'" No laughter accompanied the statement.

"Says the man who fell in love with his asset." Two could play at this game.

Mac's voice dropped an octave. "I think you better—"

He hung up on Mac with a smile before he could start his tirade about his wonderful Mara.

A long sigh didn't alleviate the fact that the night had ravaged him. He wouldn't be any good for the shoot today. Dark purple circles encased his eyes.

His skin paled from lack of sleep. Leigha's sharp perception would sense something was eating at him. She had questioned him about it last night. He couldn't go there.

In light of the new information, he decided to go to the studio early and get eyes on her. He took a cab from the upper eastside to Tribeca. A little peace and quiet would do him good before he canceled the shoot.

As the cab pulled up to the building, one of the Range Rovers sped away. His heart raced as his instincts took over. *Leigha*. He took the stairs two by two to the front door of the studio. He stopped at the landing, grabbing his Glock from his shoulder holster. The door to the studio was ajar. His heart beat wildly as silence teased him. He strained to hear anyone moving around. He pushed the door open with his foot as he pointed his gun, sweeping the room. From his angle he could see inside the closet that contained Leigha's portfolio of work. Neat piles of photos covered the floor. Not one picture remained in its binder. The configuration was odd.

He went to check out the rest of the studio. Nothing else seemed out of place. He put his gun in his holster and knelt down to start picking up the photos.

"Oh my God, what are you doing?" Leigha's hands covered her mouth and tears flowed down her cheeks without hesitation.

He stood up. "Nothing. I came in and it was like this."

"Bull. Fucking. Shit. Why would you get here this early in the morning? The sun's barely up.

My God, you look like shit." She stood back, eyes wide. "Oh my God! Are you the one who broke into my apartment? This shoot was all a set-up, wasn't it?" She turned, running down the stairs and out into the street.

He ran after her to get her under control. Charging out of the building, he saw her come undone. Her hands shook violently as she tried and missed dialing the numbers several times. "Hello? I would like to report a break-in."

He grabbed her by the shoulders.

She yelled into the phone. "Help me! He's attacking me now. Hurry. My address —" Her phone fell from her hand.

She screamed at top volume. "Let me go!"

"Goddamn it! Listen to me. I didn't do this. I came in and it was already like that. A Range Rover sped away as I drove up."

Her eyes were wild and unfocused. He had lost this battle with her. She was too far gone.

She wrestled away from him. Breathing heavily with her hands on her hips, she seemed to be trying to compose herself. He backed away with hands up, knowing it was in both their interests.

Snatching up the phone, she pressed some buttons on it. She backed away from him with uncertainty and sadness etched on her face. Her eyes never left him.

"My studio has been broken into and I know who did it. I called nine-one-one, but I don't know if the call went through." She held the palm of her hand to her forehead. Her breathing shortened. She eyed him with suspicion and fear.

Shit! He knew who she had called. His cell

phone buzzed. He turned away and answered it without a hello. "Let me—"

"What. The. Fuck." Mac sounded at the end of his rope. This case was getting to him.

"I got to the studio and someone broke into the closet. They went through her portfolios of photographs. She accused me of going through not only the studio but her apartment as well. She's unglued to say the least. Do you know something else you're not sharing?" He stood with his back to her, running his hands through his hair over and over again. His nightmare came back to life. He had failed…again.

"Sit tight. I'm on my way over there now. I'll talk to you later." Mac hung up before he could get in another word.

He put his phone in his pocket and looked over at Leigha. Tears rolled down her cheeks. Her eyes stayed on him.

———◆———

Leigha looked up to see Mac walking through a scene filled with flashing lights as a cop took her statement.

"His name is Dean Andersen. I can send you a picture because he *was* one of my models." Her body hadn't stopped shaking. Tears continued to run down her cheeks of their own freewill. Confusion reigned supreme. Even in her state of emotional unrest, things didn't add up when it came to Dean.

Mac stepped in. "Officer, can I have a word with you, please? Leigha, stay right here. I'll be back in a minute."

He walked the police officer in the direction of his car. Their heads bent toward one another as if they were conspiring together.

Within ten minutes of his conversation, police officers came out of the building, got in their cars, and left.

"What the hell is going on?" She felt on the brink of total collapse.

"I told them MBK would handle this case from here on out." His face became impassive as he tried to reassure her.

"Bullshit! I told them about Dean. They need to follow through with this and arrest him." Her voice cracked as her emotions hit overload. The ropes that bound her had given way. She hugged herself to hold it together.

"Leigha, it's not Dean." He stared at her as if he were contemplating something.

"What aren't you telling me?" Her hug tightened.

"Dean works for me. He's your detail. Yes, I know you didn't want one, but things have amped up recently." He stopped talking long enough for her to absorb the information. "I wish I could say that I'm sorry, but I'm not. You need protection."

As she went over the last couple of days, things started to click into place. The phone call, the bike ride, and his protectiveness. She was stunned and needed to apologize.

Out of the corner of her eye, she caught sight of one of the Range Rovers before it took off. "Mac! That car followed us last night but stopped halfway up the block. That's the second time I've seen it. Do you think it has anything to do with all the break-ins?"

Mac rubbed the scar above his eyebrow. "Yea, the Range Rovers belong to the Russian consulate. What the hell have you been taking photos of, Leigha?" Frustration reared its head.

"Nothing that I know of. I need to go back up and clean up the mess." Her eyes burned from tears. Goose bumps formed on her arms. She needed an escape from her life.

He rested his hands on her shoulders. "Hey, you need to calm down. I got this. You're protected. I'm sending over someone to upgrade your security system."

She sighed heavily, defeated by the day. She made her way back to her slice of heaven made into hell.

Stepping into the studio, the thin piece of twine holding her together became frayed. In the space of a couple of days, the two break-ins and a chase were mixed with fear and dread.

Dean had provided her with excitement and relief. He invaded her senses, taking up space between her hard edges. He made her uncomfortable yet intrigued her. She hadn't wanted to believe he was part of the break-ins. Mac's confirmation gave her relief.

Questions about Dean filled her head. She would be demanding answers. Her thoughts caught an image of his body. It made her tingle, which proved to further unnerve her. She was a hot mess. He wouldn't want anyone this screwed up.

She patted her forehead with the back of her

hand, scanning the interesting piles of photographs all over the floor. They had been neatly placed next to the binder, making it easy for her to put them back together. This seemed completely different than what had happened at her apartment.

"What happened?"

She jumped back. Lost in her own thoughts, she had forgotten Chloe would be coming into work. Her shaking hands clutched her chest.

"I'm sorry. I didn't mean to scare you." Worry covered Chloe's face.

"When I came in this morning, Dean was leaning over a pile of photos. I assumed he did this. Mac assured me—"

"Oh, no. There's no way Dean did this. I mean, I don't think he would do something like this." Chloe fumbled over her words.

"Mac told me Dean works for him and is my bodyguard. Is there something you want to share?" She looked at Chloe as things continued to add up.

Chloe looked down, pushing her hair behind her ear. "Mac contacted me when you said you didn't want protection. I'm sorry. As your friend, I wanted to do what was best for you. You haven't been yourself lately."

"Thank you. I actually appreciate it. I feel like I'm falling through the cracks in the floorboards sometimes. Can you help me clean this up?" She turned off her emotions before they ran roughshod over her.

They worked in silence for most of the day, organizing photos in binders and categorizing them. She sensed that Chloe had questions about

Dean but staved off asking about them. The day wore on with her emotional upheaval leveling itself off.

She and Chloe finished up in the studio as early evening turned into night. The lights of the surrounding buildings reflected off the river, making them look like ghosts underwater. Anxiety always took hold in her chest as darkness fell around the studio. The atmosphere tickled the waiting nightmare. A chill ran through her she couldn't quite explain. She spent five days a week, ten to fourteen hours a day in her studio, but tonight she wanted to leave and go back to her apartment on the Upper West Side.

They left together, walking out into the crisp night air.

"Are you going to be all right? You've been dealing with a lot lately."

Chloe's concern tugged at her. She was so much more than an assistant. She had turned into a real friend that cared about her.

"I've been feeling off ever since Cancun. Something's not right, but I can't pinpoint where it's coming from. I guess I'll have to ride it out. I'll see you tomorrow. And thanks again." She gave her a hug, wishing she could tell her more. Remembering and talking through the details might help her to understand and piece things together. She would have to wait to exhale to release the nightmare.

Chloe nodded and turned, leaving her standing on the sidewalk. She wrapped her coat tight around herself as the chill in the air groped her. She had tolerated groping for years. Her tolerance had run out, putting her on the other side of the camera.

Sirens rang out from far away. Steam wisped up through the manhole covers in the dark street. She took out her camera, spotting the perfect opportunity to take a snapshot of the street scene. Programming it to keep the shutter open meant she needed to set the camera on a tripod. She pulled out a small one with retractable legs. The perfect height for the ground level shot. After many shots at different angles, weariness threatened to take over. She packed up her stuff and hailed a cab home instead of taking the subway.

The cab had the familiar smell of stale cigarettes. It jolted and jerked its way through the streets of Manhattan. She scrolled through the pictures on her camera and came across the ones of Dean at the beach. His eyes gave away his struggles and heartache even as he tried to hide it. She was beginning to understand him. He was little boy lost without an anchor. Her heart ached for him. She knew something about being lost.

Her breath fogged the window. The city displayed contrasts from old and modern, grimy and sleek. The dichotomy was a photographer's dream, as she tended to see everything through the lens of a camera with angles, apertures, and lighting. Opposites always led to chaos in a big city. Yet the city managed to run in an orderly manner. Crime made the headlines every day, but she always felt safer here than anywhere else in the world.

They pulled up to her building, a classic early 1900s style with a stone front and generous beveled glass entry doors. Her papa invested in the building years ago and gave her the apartment as a gift for her twentieth birthday. He gave an apartment to each of his daughters. The gesture felt less like a gift and more of an obligation for him.

She peered out the window at the strangers on the street. Her heart pounded in her chest. Feeling afraid made her angry. She shoved the money at the cab driver and ran up the stairs. The doorman tipped his hat as she rushed into the lobby to catch an elevator. She breathed out, relieved to have made it to the elevator unscathed. What had her life become?

The inside of her apartment reflected her modern clean lines and edges, a contrast to the antique exterior of the building. One light shone in the living room, leaving the rest of the apartment cast in darkness. She walked to the kitchen on the Persian wool rugs she had added to soften the lines.

She stood in her state of the art kitchen. The glossy black and white subway tile, black mica countertops, and white cabinets belonged in a magazine. Her life had become one façade after another. Memories of baking filled her head. Baking used to bring her peace, but baking for one lost its appeal. An island onto herself, she had chosen to reside there in her lonely existence. Happiness eluded her.

Thoughts of sleep pulled her down the dark hall to her bedroom. She continued on, having lost her appetite to eat a light store bought frozen dinner.

Exhaustion took over as she dropped her bags

at the end of the bed. Dean took up the space in her head. Closing her eyes, she visualized him on the beach as excited energy traveled through her body. A smile pulled at her lips. The image of him became her escape from reality. Wild thoughts raced through her mind. It had been a while and she needed some relief.

Being naked always gave her freedom. She took pride in her body and loved the feel of the cold air on her naked skin. Her hands roamed over her body as she cupped her sex, lightly tracing her seam. She gasped at her wetness from just thinking about him. She grabbed her favorite vibrator from her nightstand. Lying back on her bed, she played with her breasts, seductively sliding the toy between her legs. She closed her eyes. Only one man could satisfy her tonight. Her pull to him wouldn't be denied.

CHAPTER 10

Leigha imagined his hands on her, taking control, pinning her wrists above her head. Her eyes shot open as questions spiraled in her head. When had she ever wanted someone else to take control, especially him? Stunned by the image, she took shallow breaths as she tried to follow her thoughts.

The doorbell rang, startling her already fragile state. Bolting upright, she tossed the vibrator on the nightstand and grabbed a silk robe from her walk-in closet. She hurried to the intercom to answer the doorman.

"Hello?" she said, out of breath.

"A gentleman by the name of Dean is here for you. Should I let him up?"

There was rustling on the other end mixed with some Australian expletives.

"Leigha, I'm not taking no for an answer. If you don't let me up, I'll find a way. We need to talk." His voice tightened.

"Fine. You can come up." She clicked off, leaving him with the coolness of her voice. He had no idea what he was in for with her. This time she would have her way. He wouldn't be bossing her around. Besides, she was still pissed as hell despite her attraction to him. He should have told her he was her detail.

She rushed to her bedroom to pull her hair up in a ponytail. Her reflection showed a woman with rosy cheeks and a sparkle in her eye. She considered leaving it down for him. Anger simmered to the surface. She wouldn't be doing anything for him. As she balled her hair up, a knock came at the door. She dropped it. Her hair fell gently around her face. Her hands clasped together hoping to rein in her emotions. He did this to her. *Damn him.*

She opened the door to a huge bouquet of flowers. Pink roses, Reuben lilies, and fuchsia littered with baby's breath filled the doorway. He hid behind them. She stepped aside so he could make his way to the living room. The door closed with a soft click. A quiet came over her. She had never received flowers from a man.

"Hello? Earth to Leigha. Are you okay?"

Heat rose to her cheeks. After her cold welcome, she thought he might come prepared for a fight. He stood waiting for an answer.

She folded her hands in front of her and whispered, "Are those for me?"

His eyes furrowed in confusion. "Of course. I felt awful about this morning. You have to believe that I had nothing to do with the break-ins." His mouth drew a taut line. He looked like he wanted to say more.

"Why pink?" She couldn't stop staring at the flowers.

"Because you like pigs. Pigs are pink, aren't they? I noticed your collection at the studio." He pushed the flowers in her direction in an ungraceful hand-off.

Her head snapped up as her eyes pinned him. Of course he noticed her pigs. He had to get a lay of the land as her bodyguard. But this was more. He saw her. Softness glowed from inside him. Her tingle amplified. Her escape had arrived.

"Yes, you're right. I do love pigs. My mama read the book *Charlotte's Web* to me when I was younger. You might say I fell in love with Wilbur. I was fascinated by the fact Charlotte and Fern saved him." She leaned in to smell the roses and lilies. "Thank you. I'll put them in water."

When she came back in the room, he had taken off his leather jacket and thrown it on a chair. His arms stretched across the back of the couch with his ankle crossed over his knee. He made himself right at home, owning the space around him. Their eyes connected and his face lit up. She never imagined having that effect on anyone. Her body was a magnet to his steel. She wanted to snuggle in beside him, making their pieces fit. The thought crossed her mind that he could take her ache away. Besides, he was the bodyguard, a short-term stint.

"I saw one of your pigs at the studio had a catastrophic event. What happened?" He challenged her.

She looked down at the hair tie she grabbed from the bedroom. "Nothing. It's a reminder of something that happened long ago." She started to gather her hair to the top of her head putting it in a bun. He bolted off the couch and grabbed her hands.

"No. I like your hair down. Leave it. Please."

Snatching her wrists out of his hands, she said, "You're awfully bossy for a model. Tell me, how long have you known Mac? And please don't say, 'Mac who?' because I know you work with him. You were assigned to be my bodyguard against my wishes, I might add. I may be blond but it doesn't mean I'm stupid. So spill it, Aussie." She crossed her arms in front of her.

He threw his head back, barking out a belly laugh. "God, you are a feisty one, aren't you? You don't miss a trick. I gotta tell ya. It's a turn on." He stood back with his hands on his hips. "You're right. I work for MBK. I was assigned to you after the break-in here." His voice took on a serious tone and his eyes turned dark. "I'm going to protect you. More importantly, I want to protect you, Leigha." The words hang in the air. "There's something bigger going on, but we're not sure what the whole picture is yet."

"Mac said the Range Rovers belong to the Russian consulate. What's that about?"

"We're not sure. Our first clue to the fact it was a professional job was the lack of fingerprints. They either hacked of your security systems here and at the studio or they had a key. We know Brock was involved with the Russian mob through CZR Investments. Now that the Russian government seems to be involved it can only mean one thing. The government is linked to one of the most powerful Russian families. The head of the family is elusive to say the least. Very few people even know what he looks like. Can you think of any reason why they want your photographs?"

Fear crept through her. Tears began to well up of their own accord. "I have no idea. I took some photos in Cancun, but that doesn't seem to be the focus. Does it?" Her fingers dug into her arms. "This is serious, isn't it?" She could barely get out the words.

His large tan hand came up to cup her face. His thumb drew a line across her bottom lip. He stared at her lips like he wanted to devour them. "Yea, this ranks right up there with international shit storm. Please keep sharing anything you can remember. I'm here to protect you. I need you to trust me. So let me." His words rolled off a gentle breath.

Protection seemed to be the thing lacking in her life. Her mama had always hovered over her in a protective way, but she never knew why. As she got older, she had chosen to fend for herself. He offered some relief. Her shoulders relaxed as her arms fell to her sides.

"I get why you didn't tell me you were there to watch out for me. By the way, are you really a model? Because you're really good." She wanted the truth before she could move forward.

"I started in modeling when I was a teenager, but it wasn't what I wanted out of life. I ran straight for the Aussie military at the tender age of eighteen and never looked back. My father is a military man and I was expected to join." A dark shadow crossed his face. "Serve and protect must be part of the DNA, but it seems that's the only thing my father and I have in common." He cast his eyes down.

"I'm sorry. I didn't mean to bring up painful memories." She stroked his cheek with her thumb. "You can trust me too, you know. It seems like you need to unburden yourself from your secrets."

His lips gave way to a faint smile. "You are most definitely not a dumb blonde."

"I just may have your number, Mr. Andersen."

"Wagner." He smiled.

"What?"

"My name is Dean Wagner. I needed a cover name. But if I'm going to get you to trust me, I need to be honest with you."

"Oh, I see it now. You look like a Wagner. I should have caught on right away." She couldn't take her eyes off him.

He laughed. "You know, my favorite movie as a kid was 'Babe.' It was the story about the pig that herded sheep. He was always in control. I think I found my nickname for you."

"That seems to fit, doesn't it?"

"You could give up a little of your control."

"I'll think about it," she said coyly. The shift toward him was ever so slight, but she felt it. If he were going to be short-term, she would make the most of it. She hoped he was on the same page.

CHAPTER 11

Her smile transformed her face, brightening her hazel eyes. Dean loved how she challenged him calling him out on his pile of crap. He found himself wanting to share part of his past he hadn't shared with anyone, ever. She might be the one to help him break through, getting rid of the guilt once and for all. But he would have her under him before then if even for a little while.

She turned him on in every way imaginable. He wanted her to willingly submit to him, to understand how beautiful giving up her tight control could be. Something tragic lurked beneath her tough exterior. She would require kindness and trust before she would give him any of herself. He would peel away the layers slowly. But how much could come out of this for the short time they would be together? Short, sweet, and to the point worked for him, but something niggled at him.

Her hand cupped his jaw as she pressed her lips to his. Unexpectedly tentative at first, she melded into the kiss. His hands held her waist as she shivered at his touch. His tongue licked at the seam of her lips. Gasping, her mouth opened and he took advantage of the moment, invading every part of her mouth. The moan from her made his body tightened with want. Even as his body wanted more, his heart put the brakes on. He was usually all in. Beautiful women had become his casual escape for no more than a couple of hours.

"Let's go to the bedroom." She laced their hands together.

As they made their way to the bedroom, he made a mental note of how her apartment looked like a museum, not a thing out of place. Lost in his observations, he crashed into her as she whipped around in front of him at the foot of the bed. She kissed him like someone who had gone without for too long. But this kiss lacked any emotion. She wanted to satisfy a need. The target was in her sights. He recognized the MO of a detached, hungry woman. But he wanted this woman wanting him, not using him. Her hands skated under his shirt over his abs as she tried to pull his shirt off. He caught her hands and looked up to find her vibrator lying on the nightstand.

"I see someone started without me." No smile accompanied the comment.

She turned her head to the place where he stared at her toy. Giggling, she covered her mouth with her hand. This was the first time he had ever heard her laugh. Her giggle lit places in him that had gone dark, catching him off guard.

She rose up on tiptoe. "Well, you were here in spirit at least. But I never did finish." Her lips crashed down on his. Her desire for release spoke to him.

He took her wrists and pulled them down. "You're not going to drown yourself in me. I won't be used to take away your ache. Do you think you can escape with a roll in the hay?" Jesus, where did that come from? He loved a good romp.

"Yes, actually I do. It works every time," she said with a smug look on her face.

Pulling her tighter to him, their bodies touched from chest to toe.

He whispered in her ear, "When I have you, you will know beyond a shadow of a doubt who's inside you as you scream my name." He waited to let her take that in. Her eyes got bigger. "You'll submit to me because you will trust me completely. You need to learn to let someone else take over, babe."

She swallowed the lump in her throat giving him a slight smile. She seemed pleased at his name for her. She had gotten too used to being in control. He wanted her to know her way wasn't always the best way, even for her.

"You did rescue me from that car trying to follow me. I do trust you." A shadow of doubt veiled her face as if she had trusted before without success.

"Then I'll reward you with pleasure." His thumbs brushed against the pulse in her wrists.

He untied her robe. It drifted off her shoulders collapsing like a magician's curtain, revealing the hidden beauty. She was spectacular and comfortable in her own skin. His eyes took her in from those hazel eyes to toned legs. He let out a sigh of relief.

Leaning down, he said, "You have the body of

a gazelle, but you're as sharp as a pig. A deadly combination. You challenge me at every turn, but we need to work together. Don't you think?"

She nodded in agreement. She stuck her chest out, begging to be touched. He had her right where he wanted her. He hoisted her up as her legs wrapped around his waist. He threw them on the bed. She buried her head in his neck. Her rapid breath made him want to lose himself in her. He kissed her mouth with all the gentleness he could muster. Her hips arched upward. He was so hard his cock could undo the zipper to his pants.

Peppering her jaw with kisses, he made his way down to her small, round breasts accented by pink, taut nipples. He kissed, licked, and bit each one, driving her higher and higher. His hand slid lower, finding her folds soaking wet.

"It seems you're more than ready." He feathered her belly with soft kisses.

"Yes...hurry."

"What's the rush?" He chuckled.

He grabbed the vibrator from the nightstand and carefully eased the tip in and out. Her hips bucked, encouraging him to put it in farther.

He nipped her hipbone. "Patience, babe."

"I don't want the fake one. I want you," she said with a ragged breath as beads of sweat formed on her chest.

"I'll decide when you get me."

He increased his rhythm as her breathing became more rapid. Adjusting his hand, his thumb stroked her clit each time he pushed in. She clamped down as he did the unthinkable and pulled out.

She sat upright. "What are you doing? You need

to finish me."

He climbed up her body and gently grabbed the back of her hair. She sucked in a breath and her pupils dilated. She enjoyed the challenge and friction between them. But he also saw fear laced in her pleasure. He let go immediately.

"Leigha, why do I see fear in your eyes? Talk to me." He moved to get off her and she grabbed him.

"I'm surprised. You're different. This is different for me. I like it."

He accepted her answer, but memories from his past crashed down around him. "Do you trust I'll take care of you?" His words strangled him. He needed to hear from her that they could continue.

"Yes. Hurry up."

He lightened the mood. "Tsk, tsk, tsk. So bossy. Bossy girls don't get to finish." He wanted to tease her a little bit.

"I'm sorry." She grabbed his hand, leading it back to where she wanted it to go.

He laughed. "I see we have a ways to go with the giving up control thing."

He set the vibrator on high bringing her back to the edge of climax and stopped once again. This time she didn't say a word. Her hands gripped the sheets to keep from trembling.

"Good babe. There may be hope for you yet. But there's a method to my madness."

He continued his rhythm, putting the toy on a low speed, increasing his in and out movements. As he felt her begin to tense, he set the speed on high, turning upward into her sweet spot.

Victory came as she screamed his name at top

volume. Her body shook and she grabbed on to his wrist, pulling it farther into her. Her mouth fell open and her body flushed the most beautiful shade of pink. She was the most beautiful sight he had ever seen. Her hips relaxed coming to a rest.

He got rid of the vibrator and climbed on top of her. She opened her eyes, glazed in lust, euphoria, and satisfaction.

"That was amazing. I've never…" She stared at him.

"You've never what? This is what happens when you let me take care of you." He kissed her forehead.

Tears sprung in her eyes. She pushed him off of her, scrambling to get off the bed. She stood in the middle of the room and wrapped her arms around her.

He knelt on the bed. She needed her space. It took everything he had not to go to her. "What happened? Please talk to me. Tell me what's going on."

"I don't know. Something triggered me. I can't explain it." She made a fist at the center of her chest as if she wanted to grab the hurt.

Her look of confusion and desperation stabbed him. He climbed off the bed and walked toward her with open arms, giving her a form of refuge. She huddled into him.

He rubbed her back. "Shh, you'll figure it out. Give yourself time. I'm here when you need me."

She reminded him of the piece of his heart he'd lost long ago to a girl who needed him.

She leaned into him as her face nestled in his neck. On a beg, she whispered, "Please stay with me tonight. I don't want the nightmare to come back."

His body tensed at her suggestion.

CHAPTER 12

His body became rigid. Another man who couldn't stand the intimacy of lying next to the woman he just got off. Leigha's head swam in the afterglow with the impulse to smack him. The men in her life either didn't want her or never stuck around. Why should she expect anything different from him? Frustration, sadness, and anger made for a potent after sex cocktail.

She pushed him away and bristled. "Fine. Whatever. God forbid you should want to do something like stay because I need you to." She never asked for anything from anyone. Suddenly she needed him, of all people. Anger took over at letting him see her weakness and vulnerability.

His body sagged as he let out an exaggerated sigh. "That's not it. I had a meeting tonight. I need to make a phone call. I'll be right back."

He walked to her and held her chin on his bent finger. "You need to understand how hard this is going to be for me tonight. I want you. But not like this. You have a secret you need to find the answer to before we can be together. I still have a job to do without distraction." A pained look came over his face.

"Here's a truth and a care for you. I know you have secrets too. They reflect in your eyes and in all the things you don't say. Looks like we both might need a confessional." She wouldn't let him off the hook. Two could play the game of who had the biggest secret.

His hand dropped as his face shut down, trying to hide his shock at her insight. He nodded and left to go to the kitchen.

She always had the inclination she would have made an excellent spy or at least CSI agent. Sneaking around had its benefits. It was how she got her treasured photograph. She tiptoed to the door and flattened herself against it. She couldn't help herself as she listened in on his phone conversation.

"Hey, mate, so I'm at Leigha's. You told me stay close and apparently that won't be a problem because I'll be spending the night." He paused. "Yea, yea. I'm *on* her. I got it the first time. She knows I work for MBK." He stopped talking. "Well, it would have been nice if you told me you told her. She's too smart for her own good. You okay? You haven't even yelled at me yet."

The long period of silence made her stomach lurch. Mac must be on the other end, giving him important information. She peeked around the corner. His shoulders folded in on themselves as he held his head in his hand.

"God, I'm so sorry, mate. I know what it's like to lose your partner. How did she die?" His voice cracked.

His words washed over her. Her skin grew

cold. She held her arms around herself sliding to the floor. *Partner. She.* He could only be talking about one person. Sydney portrayed a beautiful yet damaged creature. Wanted by both men and women, she manipulated them to get her way. Even though she wasn't in love with Sydney, her death hit her hard. Another reminder she had little to no control in the world around her as another person disappeared from her life. Grief took over as a tear slipped down her cheek. She couldn't stop the trembling.

He came around the corner and knelt down beside her. "You heard me talking to Mac."

"How?"

"They found her body floating in the Azat River in Armenia. It's a warning from the Russians. We recently confirmed her role as a double agent, working for the CIA and the Armenians, which means the Russians. She got caught in the crosshairs." He swept his thumb across her cheek to catch her tears. "Mac's not doing so great and he's a tough guy. He said he'd talk to you tomorrow. He trusts I'll take care of you." He gave her a tight smile picking her up off the floor and cradling her in his arms.

He rubbed her back and then asked, "Were you in love with her?"

She lifted her head, peering up into his non-judgmental face. His question was to gauge the extent of the TLC she would need. He showed his soft underbelly whether he knew it or not.

"No. I ache for her and Mac. I need to call Mara." She started to move away from him.

He held her tight. "No, he said not to. You can

catch up with her tomorrow. I think Mac needs her right now." His eyes were full of compassion as he wiped away more of her tears.

He crept in where she didn't want him to be. But she craved him all the same. She needed her sisters. She always talked to her sister about everything, but the dynamics had changed lately, making Mara's priorities different. The sisterly unit included Mac. Mara would no longer run to her sisters for comfort. That job belonged to Mac. Mara would be there for him. A shiver ran through her as a leg of their trifecta came loose.

"I'm exhausted physically and emotionally. Can we go to bed?" Her strength left her like a punctured tire.

The glint in his eye accompanied half a smirk. "Yeah, but I can't sleep naked tonight. I don't trust you won't attack me in my sleep and try to ravage my body."

She laughed. "You're probably right. You never know when I'll attack…again. Although there was plenty of attacking on your part."

She sauntered away from him, leaving him with the view of one of her finer assets—her ass. She worked eighteen ways to Sunday. Pulling the sheets back, she looked up to notice the huge bulge in his pants. Mission accomplished.

"Goddamn women. The bane of my existence," he muttered under his breath.

Giving her a taste of her own medicine, he stripped down to his briefs. She couldn't peel her eyes away from his body. He had the perfect build. He crawled over the sheets and kissed her firmly on the lips.

"Good night, babe. I'll be sleeping on top of the covers tonight to protect me from grabby hands." He wiggled his brows.

A piece of her hardened heart softened every time he called her babe. She laid her head on his shoulder, praying her nightmare would stay in hiding. He caressed her bare back until exhaustion finally took her.

CHAPTER 13

*D*ean's *pre-dawn* wakeup call kicked him in the leg. He turned over to find her thrashing around oddly. Her fists were down by her sides as if her arms were held by ropes. He watched intently, trying to figure out what was happening. This may be the insight to dreams that tormented her.

She started to mumble. "No. Stop. Please don't do this. It hurts. Please, Ben." Tears streamed down her face. Drops of sweat broke out across her forehead. She began sobbing on a helpless cry.

He couldn't take anymore and grabbed her by the shoulders. "Leigha, wake up. You're having a nightmare." His heart ached in his chest, thrown into the memories of his past.

She startled awake and quickly moved away from him, almost falling off the bed. He managed to grab her before she fell, pulling her to him.

"Shh, it's all right. The nightmare is over." He wiped her hair away from her wet cheeks and cradled her to him.

Silence enveloped them, taking up the space of unanswered questions.

"Babe, who's Ben?" he whispered in her hair.

Her body stiffened. She tried using her elbows to push him away.

"Please don't shut me out. I want to help you." He let her move him to arm's length. Something deep within him needed to help her to ease the remorse from his past.

"He was an ex-boyfriend. I don't know enough to share it with you yet. I need time to figure it out." Her face morphed into a pained mask of torture. She had been living with this nightmare for a while.

She stroked the fine hair on his chest. "Maybe we can talk more in the morning. I'm exhausted."

He remained silent as she turned over, giving him her back. She managed to stir his pot of guilt stew. He thought of her, the woman he couldn't save. All because she never told him what happened behind closed doors. The guilt ate at him for years, but he could never let it go. He needed to shut his thoughts down before they pulled him under. Being a master at compartmentalizing, he filed his feelings in the proper box. But his emotions clung to him like silk threads, strong enough to hold, transparent enough to see through.

He stayed vigilant, watching her sleep, wondering what secrets she held in her nightmare. She muttered every once in a while. He tried to listen to what she said, hoping to get more insight into her darkness.

After a fitful sleep, he woke to a ray of light hitting him in his left eye. The fragile gazelle next to him slept soundly without any murmuring from the night. He slid out of bed and tiptoed to the picture-perfect kitchen to find the coffee pot.

He leaned on the pristine countertop gripping his cup like an anchor. The reflective surface of the black coffee showed sad eyes. He wouldn't do this again. He couldn't stand by and watch someone else hide their pain. Maybe die because they held their secrets too close. There were so many questions she wouldn't answer. His chest tightened, remembering one of the reasons why he'd left years ago. Returning to his beloved country would bring the nightmare to life. He finished his coffee setting it in the sink. His intention was to get out of there as soon as possible. Once this shoot ended he wanted off the case. He would bury himself in work and never look back.

"Good morning." She stretched her arms over her head. Her eyes were puffy and red from the night before. "How are you doing?" She stood in front of him. He looked for cracks but there were none. She acted as if everything was normal. How long had she lived like this thinking last night was normal?

She squirmed uncomfortably in front of him. He remained silent. Her brows knitted together in concern or wonder, he wasn't sure.

"I'm fine. I have to go. I'll catch you at the studio this afternoon." He clamped his jaw so hard the muscles popped with tension.

Being an agent, you trained your face to be in stealth mode. He wished it could be different, but he already knew the outcome. Time to cut and run.

"What the hell is wrong with you?" She rested her hands on her hips, looking for a fight.

He stepped closer into her space. "Nothing's wrong with me. What about you? You come in here as if you didn't wake up with a horrible nightmare. You said you would talk about it this morning, but you have no intention of talking about it, do you?" Blood rushed through his veins, searching for an outlet for his anger and hurt.

"Oh. What? So now you're going to run away because I won't bare my soul to you or are you getting a little too close for comfort?"

That's it. Turn it back on me. Classic deflection.

He put his hands up in front of him, shaking his head. "I can't do this again. I gotta go. I'll see you later." He brushed by her, heading for the bedroom to get dressed.

She remained in the kitchen, glancing over her shoulder at him. Her features strained for understanding. Her cold mask slid into place. He rushed to the front door, making his escape.

The elevator slugged to the lobby. He burst through the front doors, running down the stairs and out onto the street. His lungs begged to take in air. He looked up at the sky and ran his fingers through his hair.

"Shit! Damn it." He needed her for so many reasons. Too scared of the fight, his flight response kicked in.

The tight box he welded together on the inside started to break apart. He built the box to hold his guilt and pain in a secure location. She held the torch burning through it. She locked her emotions away with her coldness, but her spears of passion stabbed him. Underneath her cold mask, she showed all the signs of heartache and tenderness. He wanted nothing more than to hold her to him and dissolve her pain. Something ripped inside him he needed to sew up. The need to run outweighed the need to give her comfort. He could add coward to his list. He would run until his legs gave out or he found the nearest bar, whichever came first. But he would never outrun the ghost of his past.

CHAPTER 14

Leigha stood in her empty apartment. Sadness engulfed her. A distant ticking clock was her only companion. Time had run away from her. Loneliness would break her before anything else. She flattened her hands against the wall as she crumbled to the floor.

For once in her life she needed to lean on someone. Reaching out to him had been a mistake. He instantly retracted from her. He couldn't handle being needed and shut down. She hadn't taken him for a runner, but he sprinted, triggered by something. His words "I can't do this again" imprinted themselves in her head. There were questions that needed answers. She would get them one way or another. He wasn't going to leave her in the dust without an explanation.

Her cries echoed off the empty space. The pain of not being able to share her torment speared her. She wanted to trust him, but she needed to go deeper. Life wouldn't operate on her terms anymore. She had no choice but to let go. Let fate have her way. It may be fear that really held her back.

Pain turned to anger. Pure fury bubbled to the surface. Tired of being hemmed in by her clean, straight lines without an escape, she longed to break free. The break-ins and nightmares shook her to her core, but his abandonment broke the final straw. She stood on shaking legs and swiped her arm across the countertop. Everything flew through the air without grace or pattern.

She ripped open the cabinets, smashing the plain white plates onto the tile floor. She grabbed anything in her way, decimating an entire row of dinnerware. Her panting filled the air as if she had been running for miles. She took stock of her heap of anger broken on the floor. The music of shattered porcelain released something in her. Surrounded by the jagged points of anger, she braced herself on the counter. They would cut anything it their path. A calm took over and her frustration dissolved. Determined not to clean up, she walked around the angry edges into her bedroom.

Her tantrum had taken a toll on her spirit, leaving her with no energy or motivation to run. Instead, she took a shower and got dressed for the day. She stopped long enough to take a long look at herself in the mirror. Where had she disappeared to for so long? Her memories of her modeling years were filled with laughter and light-heartedness. The darker side didn't seem so dark at the time, too young to know the difference.

From the time she was old enough to guess the purpose of a camera, she loved to be put on display. She would play dress-up and smile for the camera in a carefree manner. Those memories receded into a fog so dense she couldn't see them. The blurred nightmare ended that chapter of her life. Ben, her first boyfriend and photographer, seemed to be the key to unlocking the memory holding her hostage.

She moved as if underwater, making her way to the studio. Would Dean show up for the shoot? He left unhinged. She didn't know him well enough to know what his go-to would be.

When she entered the studio, the clean, neat lines assaulted her again. The anger caught her off guard. She slammed the door.

Unaware of Chloe's presence, she saw someone jump.

"I'm sorry. I didn't know you were here."

"Jesus, Leigha, you scared the crap out of me. What's going on?" Chloe's eyes grew wide.

"Dean. Or maybe it's me. Hell, it could be both of us." She threw her bag on the counter. Everything flew out. She'd be damned if she cleaned it up.

Chloe's brows rose. "Men have a way of doing that sometimes."

The studio door opened as Mara and Mac walked in. Mac's hands were stuffed in his pockets. His head hung low.

"Hey, how are you doing?" Mara rushed over to give her a hug. She gripped on for dear life.

Mara pulled away with tightened eyes and asked, "What's going on? Cuz I don't think your puffy red eyes have anything to do with Sydney. And what's with the purse on the counter?"

"Dean spent the night and we fought this morning. He left in a hurry. He couldn't wait to get away from me." She choked on the last word of truth. "Screw the purse."

"Whoa! So you're seeing Dean?"

Everyone turned as the door shut again. Raquelle strolled in like she was on the catwalk.

"Hey, Queen L, what's the word?" Dressed in a burgundy cape like overcoat, skinny pants, and sky-high stilettos, she resembled a model out of Vogue.

Mara put her hands on her hips. "She was telling me about Dean."

"Who's Dean? And why am I not in the loop?" Raquelle said with a cut in her voice.

"Apparently, I'm not seeing Dean and now you're in the loop. But he told me about Sydney." She turned to Mac. His face was pale accented by dark rings around his eyes. "I'm so sorry about what happened. Her death shocked me."

"Shocked you? Let's recap. She was my partner for many years, had my back at every turn, and saved my life on many occasions. She goes dark, turns up face down in a river. Oh, yeah, my ex-partner? Turns out she acted as a double agent for the Russians. Shocking doesn't even begin to describe the situation." He sighed heavily and wandered into the kitchen for a cup of coffee. She guessed it wasn't his first of the day.

Mara put her arm around Leigha. "Don't take his comments personally. He's having a really hard time. Turns out Sydney tipped off the Russians about Brock in Mexico. That's the latest so far."

"Holy shit! So your choices in the partners department are interesting. She basically killed Brock and saved Mara's life. The whole thing is strange. Do you have some coffee?" Raquelle wrapped it up in a few sentences. She carried on to her next point of interest, following Mac into the kitchen.

"God, if she wasn't my sister, I would strangle her. Thank God she doesn't know the half of it." Mara blew out a breath.

Leigha's head felt foggy and unclear. "Sydney was a complex person. She seemed to be caught between her conscience and her job."

"What happened with Dean?" Mara said in a soft voice.

"He witnessed one of my nightmares and questioned me about it. He got angry when I wouldn't share it with him. More pieces are coming out. But there isn't much for me to tell. I've lived with it for so long that it's become a part of my existence. I need to get a handle on it before it destroys me from the inside out. And I really need Dean because this is all too much for me. What the hell do the Russians want with me?" Tears formed when she thought she didn't have any left.

Mara folded her into her arms. No words were needed.

Mac returned with a hot brew in hand. "Mara, we gotta go. I've got a meeting downtown. Leigha, I'm sorry about Sydney and I apologize for coming across a little brash. This case has me off my game. It's not a place I like to be. Sorry Dean's being such a wanker. He needs to pull his shit together. You need him."

"Stop. You don't owe me an explanation. You've been through enough in the last couple of months. And you're right. I do need him. More than he knows."

"Aye. We have all been through it. I need to wrap this case up."

They turned to leave as Raquelle plopped herself on a stool. "So, Dean. Spill it." Questions floated in Raquelle's eyes.

Chloe joined them.

"There's nothing to tell. He works with Mac and was put on protection detail after the break-in at my apartment. We had a disagreement this morning and he left without saying a word."

Raquelle stared at her as she blew on her coffee. "So, you're sleeping with him."

"No," she said tersely.

"But he spent the night," Raquelle continued on, unfazed by her irritation.

"Yes."

"And what about the nightmares?"

She let out a sigh. "Mara told you. I really don't know what they are about, but once I do I will let you know." She didn't know how to get rid of them.

"I know I'm not getting the whole story, am I? Well, that's fine." She got up and stood in front of her. She held her hands and said, "I'm always here for you. I get that I'm flighty, but I'll drop everything for one of my sisters. I love you both."

Leigha almost broke apart from her sister's tenderness. Showing her sisters tenderness and support was usually her department. But Raquelle stepped up to lend her a shoulder to cry on. It would be a relief to hand herself over to someone and let them take over.

Raquelle hugged her and sauntered toward the door, off to her next conquest. "By the way, Dean might be a keeper," she said without turning around.

Chloe sat quietly watching the scene. "So now tell me what's really happening with Dean."

"I don't know. He's different from anyone else I've met. I feel different around him. But he has his secrets too. He wanted all the gory details of my nightmare this morning. I'm not ready to tell him. I'm not sure he's coming in to finish the shoot." She ran her trembling hand across the top of her head.

"He'll come around. He's a professional. Let's step up for the shoot at least." Chloe covered Leigha's hand with her own and squeezed. "I'm here if you need to talk or vent."

They spent the rest of the day setting up for the third bike in the set. The purple matt finish accented the chrome dragon's head to tail. The smaller size appealed to her. She wondered if the bike had been designed for a woman.

The afternoon bled into the early evening. She sent Chloe home. Both of them didn't need to be sitting around waiting for a no show.

She made herself a cup of white tea and stared out the window. The orange glow of the sunset peeked around the edges of the buildings but never touched the water. She wondered about Sydney's life and what led up to how she ended up dead in a river.

Lost in thought, her eyes traveled down to the street where she spotted two Range Rovers parked end to end. Her heart sped up at the sight of them. The quiet of the studio exploded with the slamming of the door. Her favorite teacup fell from her hands, shattering on the floor. She shook uncontrollably from head to toe.

CHAPTER 15

Anxiety had a death grip on Leigha's chest. The last of daylight streaked through the window, grasping for something to light. It found him.

"How can I protect you when you can't even lock the friggin' door?" Dean's bellow filled the empty space of the studio.

He stumbled into the kitchen. He braced himself on the counter with a bottle of Macallan hanging from the other hand. The smell the alcohol mixed with his intoxicating citrus smell wafted off him. His eyes told a story of anger and hurt under an alcohol induced haze. He was tipsy, well on his way to drunk.

She regrouped quick enough to want him to feel the coldness flow off her like dry ice vapor. Her arms crossed and legs apart, she presented a false image of bravery despite the broken cup at her feet.

"How nice of you to show up. You could have at least been professional and called." She wouldn't let him get away with it, fighting him all the way.

He ignored the dig and smirked. "Grab a couple

of your finest teacups and let's drink."

She hesitated at first. Fear skated under her skin. This man was unfamiliar to her. She reached up, carefully placing two teacups on the counter. She waited for him to pour the scotch, standing at a distance.

Even in his state, his pants strained. His cock wanted to come out and play. She reveled in what she did to him. Her hand covered up her smile. He cursed under his breath.

"I'm sorry. I didn't hear you. Were you apologizing for being an asshole this morning?" She leaned against the counter with a hand on her hip.

Her gloves were off. She was done playing around with him. Sparring bare knuckled was her preference. He stood up straight but made no move toward her.

"I'm not apologizing for this morning. I came by to see if you're ready to talk about your nightmares." He never took his eyes off her throwing back the scotch without flinching. "Come on, babe, drink. You need to catch up." He smiled like a feral jackal looking for his prey's weakness.

Her posture became rigid. Not to be outdone, she downed the scotch, her resting bitch face back in place. "I can hold my own. You'll end up on the floor long before me." Her eyes pierced him. The air hummed with intensity. He didn't look away.

He took a step forward into her space, but she didn't waver. She would never be intimidated by the likes of him.

Grabbing her cup, he poured more scotch. "Truth. You need more liquor if we are ever going to have our confessional." Her lips sealed the cup as she drank it to the bottom.

"That's my girl. Let it free you."

She closed her eyes as her body became lax.

He reached out to take her hair down, pin by pin. Her hand stroked his forearm like a kitten rubbing up against its owner. He nuzzled his nose in her hair, grabbing fistfuls of it. She didn't stiffen under his touch this time.

"I need my fix of home. The sweet smell of gardenias always brings me back to thoughts of my mother. Her gardens were always the talk of the neighborhood. The gardenias grew wild. She wrestled with them when needed, always coming inside covered in their intoxicating scent." His voice hitched at his broken distant memories.

He released her hair. He pushed her jacket off her shoulders, letting it drop to the floor. He offered her some of the numbing liquid, this time straight from the bottle. Heat rose to her cheeks and not from the alcohol.

When she opened her eyes again, they felt lazy, numbed with the haze of alcohol. Her pain began to slip away.

"I would say you are trying to get me drunk." She swayed to one side as he caught her arm.

He pressed his forehead to hers. "Babe, you do things to me I can't explain. I want you so damn much, but I can't live with secrets. I lived with them for too long." A glassy sheen covered his eyes. "A secret got someone I loved killed."

He put his finger over her lips, keeping her

questions at bay. He traced her lower lip with his thumb and up her cheek. Despite the alcohol that had soaked in, pain emanated from his eyes, but his tears never fell.

She put her hand over his and with pleading eyes said, "Please tell me more."

He bent down to kiss her gingerly on the lips. "Once I tell you, you'll change your mind about me. I don't know if I want to risk that."

He searched her face, looking for judgment. She was curious if his secret could be worse than hers, even if she didn't fully know hers yet.

"But I'm not here to talk about me. You're hiding something. I see it in your eyes and sense it in your body. I won't miss those clues again. Your nightmare affects you very deeply, maybe even changed who you are. It eats away at you underneath the surface. I watch you shut down, holding onto your control with a death grip. I want to be with you but only with complete honesty. You fight me at every turn, which friggin' turns me on. But at the same time, I need you to let me in. Otherwise, this ends and I won't turn back."

He had given his ultimatum. His eyes darkened, indicating there would be no wiggle room in the discussion. Maybe, for once, she could reach out to someone and ask for the help she needed. She had always been everyone's rock. The time had come for someone else to be the rock.

"I'll tell you my secret as soon as I figure out my nightmares. You think I don't want to be free of this? It controls me." She sniffled, trying to put her tears back in place.

"I may be able to help you unravel it. Come

with me. I want you to see something."

He grabbed her hand, lacing their fingers together. Intensity fired through her veins as she allowed the connection to deepen between them. He stood behind her in front of a full-length mirror.

"Look at your face. Look how open and soft it is. You look relaxed and at ease. Keep in mind you can't be drunk every day." He smiled. "I like when you laugh. You have a right to be happy."

She hadn't been happy in quite some time. The woman in the mirror looked like her soul had opened up. Her eyes appeared wide and bright. She hadn't felt this relaxed in…she couldn't remember. Her tight daily schedule kept everything in line and focused. He allowed her to color outside her lines, blurring her focus. The alcohol had done its job, allowing her to let go. She could forget about the nightmare and the straight lines she'd drawn, boxing herself in.

"I bet you were an awesome model. I would love to photograph you with the bike. I think it could use a woman's image, especially the purple bike. I want to capture you like this, free and open." He peppered her neck with soft kisses. He stared at her in their reflection.

"I was thinking the same thing about the purple bike. I was also thinking about getting a little racy. It's been a while since I've been in front of the camera." Her body locked up. Something poked at the back of her mind.

He turned her around to face him. "Hey, we'll go slow. Feel the bike. Do what makes you comfortable. I bet you possess exquisite lingerie."

Running his finger down her neck and between her breasts left a trail of warmth. For once, she wanted to experience life without thinking. Just feel. Let him take control and give her freedom from her cage.

"Looks like you already set up for your shot. Let me grab a camera and the Macallan." He wiggled his brows.

He picked out a camera. She grabbed the scotch, wanting to sink into her ocean of freedom. She swam freely without past memories and confines of her rigid life. Maybe she would drink more often if this was the result. She hadn't been drunk in a very long time.

"Stand next to the bike but in front. We'll start there."

She wasn't sure how steady his hand would be given how unsteady he was on his feet. Her giggles bounced around the space between them and he started to laugh with her.

"Now, straighten up, Ms. Luccenzo. Act professional."

She stood up at attention, almost losing her balance and falling on the bike. The alcohol had lubricated her veins and mind. Things became blurry and undefined. She couldn't grip onto anything in the situation.

Embracing the fun of the moment, she began taking off her clothes as she heard him snap away.

"Goddamn gorgeous is what you are. Your portfolio must be incredible. God created you for me." The camera hid his face as he focused on her through the lens.

His words spurred her on making her feel more

adventurous. She straddled the bike, pushing her chest out, clad in her black lace bra and panties. As she pushed her strap off her shoulder something felt off. She got dizzy.

Her head fell in her hands. She breathed deeply, trying to get her bearings.

"Ben, I don't want to. This isn't a good idea. If these photos go public, my career is over."

"Hey, doll, it's just you and me. Let me get you something to drink."

"Hey, are you with me? You look incredible, but you don't have to take it any farther. Don't forget this is your camera. You can do what you want with the pictures." Dean's voice pierced her alcohol-induced fog.

She meekly let out, "Okay."

The slight tremble in her hands confused her, but like a puppet she pushed the other strap of her bra down. Why was she doing this?

Snap, snap, snap. Confusion took over, blurring the lines between the past and the present. Her head got heavy as she got woozy.

"Leigha?" His voice was urgent.

He put down the camera and came to her side, helping her off the bike. His arms wrapped around her.

"Stop. Ben. Don't do this."

"Come on. You and I have wanted this for months. Come with me."

She could barely move as he scooped her up. He took her into the dark room and laid her on the floor. His hands release her breasts from the bra and he roughly fondled her. They had fooled around before, but his urgency felt different. The light washed them in red as he trapped her with his body. The smell of his high-priced cologne filled her nose. His body weighed her down.

"Leigha, you know you want this. Stop being such a cocktease. I gave you something to relax you."

She went to push him off her but couldn't move her arms or legs. She drifted in and out of consciousness. Each time there were less and less clothes between them.

"You should be wet for me. You have been before. This will be so good."

Her eyes snapped open as he shoved his way inside of her. She opened her mouth to scream as his hand slammed over it. The pain was unbearable. Three thrusts and he was done. He fell on top of her, panting in her ear.

"Stop. Get off of me, Ben!" she screamed, kicking and punching Dean.

He released her immediately trying to keep her from hurting herself without touching her.

"It's me. Leigha, it's Dean," his voice echoed loudly.

She had worked her way into the far corner. Sobs wracked her body. Curled up in the fetal position, she held her head in her hands, covering her face.

He offered her a glass of water, sitting a few feet away from her, waiting for her to calm down.

She lifted her head. Confusion and hurt were etched on his face. "I remember everything."

"What happened? Tell me. Let me be here for you," he begged her.

"When I was a model, I met this photographer, Ben. We fooled around a little, but he wanted more and I didn't. I wasn't ready. One night, he talked me into taking my clothes off. I didn't want to, but he was older and persuasive. I remember him saying he gave me something to help me relax. Then he took me into the dark room." She shook her head back and forth, looking at the door of her dark room. She always avoided it like the plague. The pieces started to snap together.

He approached her like he would a scared animal. He peeled off his shirt and gently put it over her head.

"Let me hold you."

He crawled in behind her, holding her between his legs. His arms wrapped around her in a cocoon. She trembled violently from head to toe. He rocked her slowly from side to side.

"Shh, it will get better from here. I got you."

She let go in shuttering breaths as her body began to release the angst.

Her voice cracked. "You have to understand. My father thought my modeling was silly. I never did connect with him. He didn't want me. He seemed to think I lacked creativity. His detachment made me fell like I really didn't belong in the Luccenzo family. My mama hovered over me more than the other two, but I never understood why. I was unsettled and alone. When my modeling took off, I traveled all over the world with the same group of people who came and went from my life. I bonded with them. They became my family, in a way. I trusted them and felt safe with them. Ben was a photographer I had worked with many times. We had formed a relationship of sorts. You know, older man, younger, naive woman. He ripped that all away from me when he...he raped me. The drugs must have buried the memory."

Saying the words made her nightmare a reality. She didn't know what to do with this or where to compartmentalize it. Where did this fit in?

She cried in his arms. He was her only form of refuge as she tried to wrap her head around her newfound information.

"Now I'm the keeper of your secret. The alcohol must have triggered the memory you suppressed. I'm so sorry that happened to you. It wasn't your fault. Don't ever think that." He gently kissed her temple and neck for reassurance.

His hold on her came across as protective and gentle. She thought she heard him say, "God, not again." But would he want her after knowing her secret?

They sat there in silence for a while. Her trembling body began to calm down. With each of his kind words, she sank deeper into him, molding into his body.

"How about I escort you home?" He rubbed her arms.

"Will you stay with me tonight?" she asked tentatively, afraid of the answer.

"I wouldn't have it any other way. I don't know about you, but I'm exhausted. It's been a long day and we've got a shoot tomorrow."

"What's your secret?" she whispered.

He stopped rubbing her arms. "I think we've had enough reveals tonight, babe. Mine can wait. Let's focus on you."

The relief felt like a balloon letting go of its air. She would keep pressing him. But tonight she could stay wrapped in him, hoping to wake up a changed soul.

CHAPTER 16

*D*ean *could tell* she was starting to fade. He stopped short at the kitchen. Broken dishes littered the kitchen floor.

"Someone got pissed," he said. "You want to tell me about it?"

"You might say this was the perfect storm where the past meets the present. Living with such control gets tiring." She tried to smile but failed.

"Yeah, but at least now you know why." He grabbed her into a tight hug. "You were so young and trusted someone who stole everything from you, including your control." His voice hitched as he held her even tighter. This was all so familiar. Sofia. God, why didn't he see it?

He could feel her questions rising to the surface. She tried to let go, but he held on. "Don't ask. Not now."

She held him, stroking his back. His secrets spiraled around them.

"I'll clean this up tomorrow." He needed to tuck away his emotions for later.

She led him by the hand to her bedroom. Exhaustion had taken over. He had planted the seed of suspicion. She would want to be the keeper of his secret.

She peeled her clothes off and fell into bed. The strong, confident woman retreated within the broken one before him. Relief washed over him at finally knowing her secret. But he didn't know how to make it better for her as it stirred up his past.

He shucked out of his clothes and crawled in behind her, cradling her to him. She fell asleep right away while he stroked her arms. They fell asleep entwined in each other. Her trust in him was paramount. She might heal him if he let her.

He woke up with a headache. Alcohol and adrenaline didn't make for a great combination. His body responded to the curves of the sensual woman in his arms. He was in his usual state, large and in charge. His cock nestled between her butt cheeks, warm and snug. He needed to move away from her intoxicating heat. She moved her ass back, seeking his warmth. He gasped and she laughed. Her laugh warmed him in places that had gone arctic.

"Oh, you think that's funny." He tickled her ribs.

She laughed while thrashing around, pretending to want to escape from him. She flipped around to face him and grabbed what she wanted, stroking him up and down.

He let out a groan, loving her firm hands on him. She added the right amount of pressure.

"I want you inside me." Her husky morning voice turned him inside out.

"Not yet. Don't you think you need to take

time to absorb what you've discovered? Last night was a lot to handle. We've got time. I don't want to rush you." His fingertips brushed stray blond strands from her eyes.

She looked at him for a minute but didn't disagree. Sadness came back to her eyes. The wanting almost killed him, but she needed to be ready for what he wanted and needed from her. A devious smile formed on her lips.

"You make a good point. But I have something else in mind." Her eyes were coy.

She reached behind her into the drawer in the nightstand pulling out a bottle of lubricant.

"You might as well save yourself the trouble. A woman's never gotten me off with a hand job." He threw down the gauntlet, putting his hands behind his head.

"Interesting. Well, I guess there's a first for everything."

Her hair fell to one side as she tilted her head. It spilled down the pillow, the perfect combination of naughty and nice.

"You definitely cannot back down from a challenge, can you?" He couldn't remember the last time he laughed and had this much fun. Time had gotten away from him. Memories were buried deep with his happiness.

"You like it when I challenge you." A smirk complimented her lusty eyes.

She straddled him stroking him up and down. She gripped him the way he would grip himself. Using both hands, she worked him, occasionally grabbing his balls so he didn't come too fast. He threw his head back in surrender to the goddess determined to get him off. Gripping her thighs, he rocked into her warm hands, creating the friction that would lead to his high. The tension in his body began to build. She cupped the head while stroking him all the way down and back up again. His head hit her hand over and over again. This hand job outdid every one before it. His eyes never strayed from hers. Their connection deepened. Most women were tentative, afraid of hurting him. But not his girl. She proved who was boss.

His girl? He stopped moving in mid-stroke and stared at her. She had revealed herself in so many ways. Yet, he revealed very little. She was a game changer.

"What's wrong?" Worry and insecurity showed in her eyes.

"You're so brave." He placed his hands over hers. "It never felt this good." He let go and she continued.

Her eyes locked on his in a moment of understanding. He gripped the sheets as he came all over her hands while she slowed her strokes. He shuttered, coming down from his high. The word babe left his lips.

"So I guess it was good for you." She gave him a curious smile.

"Where the hell did you learn to do that?" he said, out of breath.

"Porn. My last boyfriend made me yawn in bed. I thought the problem was me. I studied porn to learn some moves." She wiggled her eyebrows.

He threw his head back and laughed. "Well, you're an excellent student." He sat up, inches away from her face. "Truth and let me be crystal clear. You'll only ever use all your moves on me."

She grabbed some tissues to clean him up. After tossing the tissues, she cradled his face with her hands. She tilted her head sideways and said, "Umm, we'll see about that." She jumped off him and started to make a run for the kitchen, stopping at the doorway.

He moved faster, catching her around the waist from behind, pinning her back to his front. He cupped her sex, running his finger through her wet folds.

"Do you think another man can make you this wet without touching you?" She made his head spin and blood rushed through his body.

His finger circled her clit. She arched her back letting out a moan like a cat in heat. He released her, giving her a swat on the ass. "Well, that's enough for today. We need to go to the studio and finish up."

She sucked in a breath. "Payback's a bitch."

He got a good look at her ass with hair ruffled and rose-tinted skin as she made her way to the shower. The desire to be inside her took hold. He was starting to get hard again. He'd never been with a woman who made him this crazy. Crazy felt good.

CHAPTER 17

Leigha reflected on the truth of her nightmare. She had been young, naïve, and stupid. All these years, the nightmare had stayed at bay because her subconscious couldn't face the ugliness. She didn't want to face it. Now that it had revealed itself, her mind and body felt rested as if they had gone years without sleep.

The shower washed away the dirty memories. Warm water flowed down her body as some of the hurt from her past rippled over her skin. She questioned if she'd ever be truly free of the memory of her rape. She forced herself to remember the scene of the crime.

The morning after the assault became clearer. She had woken up fully clothed on the couch in his studio. Completely disoriented, her head had felt heavy. Confusion had taken over. The urgency to leave gripped her as she gathered her belongings. She would never be coming back. She had fought to recall the details of what had happened the night before. Ignoring the pain between her legs, she had assumed Ben got a little rough. Shortly thereafter, she left modeling altogether. The job didn't hold the appeal it once had for her. She couldn't explain why. But she never heard from Ben again. He seemed to have disappeared off the face of the earth.

She stepped out of the shower, her soul cleaner than ever before. Finding out about the nightmare turned her inside out. But relief came in knowing the truth. The prodding and poking at her from her subconscious wasn't there anymore.

Her outfit for the day included a deep purple dress and kitten heels. She smiled at herself in the mirror and left her hair down. The healing color of purple suited her. She sauntered into the clean kitchen and stopped dead in her tracks.

He stood on the other side of the counter covered in flour. The smell of coffee permeated the air. The kitchen looked like a pastry bomb had gone off. A light dusting of flour replaced broken pieces of the dishes.

"Hey, babe. I made breakfast. Hope you like blueberry pancakes." He smiled from ear to ear, like a little kid for his proud mama.

"I take it you like to cook with your whole body." She laughed at him, surprising herself by not getting upset over the mess. "Blueberry pancakes happen to be my favorites. I haven't had them in forever."

Ordinarily, she preferred her foods not touching. The blueberry pancakes brought back memories from her childhood. The fingers of loneliness started to lose their grip on her.

"I needed to make a run for supplies this morning. You need to get some real fresh food. The frozen stuff will kill you." He placed two near perfect, round pancakes on her plate with a pat of butter and confectioner's sugar. "How do you like your coffee?"

"I only drink white tea," she said apologetically.

"Coming right up." Unfazed by her request, he set the flame under the kettle.

He moved around the kitchen like he owned it. The air lightened and the energy flowed naturally between them. He brought her tea as if he had done it every day and sat down next to her with his coffee. She hadn't touched her pancakes.

"So, the plates? I get the feeling there's more to the story." He stared, willing her to share a little bit more.

"I got pissed off at everything, including you. It felt freeing to break something. I needed a breakthrough. I guess I got more than I bargained for. Last night changed me." Her confidence covered the lingering questions she had about herself. She spent years covering her shiny balloon in crinkled papier-mâché.

His total focus was on her. "You had every right to be angry with me." His eyes filled with sorrow and regret. "Sometimes I do before I think. I'm sorry." He took a sip of coffee. "Is that how the pig got broken at the studio? You got angry?"

Her head fell forward. "No. Ben gave me that pig. I smashed out of anger and hurt when I realized I would never see him again."

He reached out and stroked her forearm with his hand. "Well, now you know the real reason for your anger and hurt."

"Can you do me a favor?"

"Anything."

"Ben disappeared completely as in no one ever heard from him again. Can you do a search and find out what happened to him? I have no idea why I care other than it might put some more closure on this."

"Sure. But I have to be honest. I really don't give a rat's ass what happened to him. But I get the closure thing." His eyes darkened sitting with a straight back.

He took a huge chunk of pancake and stuffed it in his mouth. He looked like a kid who hadn't eaten in days with his cheeks stuffed with food. She started to laugh until tears formed in her eyes.

He wiped his thumb across her cheek to catch the tears. Concern filled his eyes as he whispered, "Are you okay?"

"Thank you." Her tears were that of gratitude as she leaned her chin on her hand.

"For what?" he said with a stuffed mouth.

"For being there for me."

He swallowed his food and looked away as if he didn't want her to see something in his eyes.

"Things are easy and comfortable with you. It scares me. A lot. I like when you challenge me. You don't let me control everything. Truth. It's kind of a relief. You better be careful. I could get used to it."

Raquelle's word 'keeper' echoed in her head.

"Well, who would've thought my babe would ever admit to that." He hesitated. "I need to stop by the office today before we shoot." He got up and started taking plates to the sink. She let the 'my babe' part slide.

"Sounds good. I need to set up. Then spend some

time with my sisters to fill them in on everything. We made a promise to always keep each other in the loop, especially after what happened in Cancun." She wasn't looking forward to sharing her bombshell. The exposure unsettled her.

"I have some questions about Cancun. You can fill me in later. Since then, Mac has been over the moon for your sister. The sun rises and sets on her ass. I can't imagine any man would want to be like that." He winked.

His playfulness warmed her. He seemed to have the key to her lock. He made her happy. A comfortable silence enveloped them.

They finished getting ready for the day. After saying goodbye, he left her alone in her apartment. This time she didn't feel cold and lonely. Part of the floor was still covered in flour. She let it go. Would she ever really be able to completely let go and give someone else control? Time would tell. She enjoyed the energy he brought with him. It balanced her and warmed her cold places on the inside.

Those feelings left as anticipation set it. She didn't know what awaited her at lunch with her sisters.

CHAPTER 18

Indian summer had arrived with a warm breeze. Fall would seek out the last blast of warmth before the November rains bore down on the city. Leigha cast her face to the sun. Her sisters chose an outdoor cafe down in the Village for their lunch date. She picked a table close to the windows, away from the street. Still nervous about the Range Rovers, she didn't want to make herself an obvious target.

Her face absorbed the warm rays of the cloudless day. She sensed her siblings nearby. Up the street two beautiful women were laughing, walking arm in arm. They had no idea she was about to rock their world.

"Hey, sister, what's up? You look very rosy, almost like you're having sex or something. And your hair is down? What do you think, Mar?" Raquelle never let anyone get away with having sex and not acknowledging it.

"Yeah, your eyes are bright and you're glowing. Looks like someone needs to spill the beans." They laughed while she remained quiet.

"I wish that was all I came here to tell you. You

two better sit down and order. Then I need to share my story with you."

Their faces fell, becoming sober. They looked at each other with anticipation plunking themselves in a chair on either side of her.

The tension grew between them as they scanned the menu to order. Their eyes peered over the menu to check her out.

Her appetite waned since making her announcement. Several times her hand went to smooth down the strands of hair that might escape the absent bun. The new her wanted to wear her hair down, but it was throwing her off. She still felt like her old self with her sisters.

Once the waiter left, they sat in silence. Mara and Raquelle exchanged glances, waiting for her to start her tale.

She stared down at her laced fingers. "When I was modeling I was part of a group of people that traveled together to photo shoots. You need to understand those people became my family." Her fingers played with the edge of the plate in front of her.

Raquelle interrupted, "You were never around much growing up. I remember missing you terribly." Her eyes squinted together.

"I never felt part of the family. Papa and I were never close. I think we all have our issues with him. But he made me feel like an outcast and unwanted. Modeling became a blessing for me in so many ways. I was happy and carefree." She folded her hands in her lap, clasping them together. Biting her lower lip, nausea rolled through her at the thought of telling her sisters her horror. She always possessed the strength among them. Her story would reveal her weakness. Telling them became harder, knowing her past would bring them pain.

"Does this have something to do with the nightmares?" Mara's eyes tightened.

Her vision became liquid glass. She pushed forward to uncovered her secret. "Yes. I finally discovered what they were about. My mind hasn't been so willing to bring that dark night into the light." She hesitated, sitting back in her chair, searching for strength.

Mara and Raquelle focused on her. Tears crested in her eyes. She rarely cried in front of them, especially as an adult. But she needed them more than ever.

She recounted the story about Ben. Her nerves pricked under her skin. Her breath shuddered, waiting for their reaction to her life-altering event.

They enclosed her in their Italian family hug, soothing her with words of care and concern. Floodgates released the pain buried deep for so long. The twine holding her together broke, shredding completely. Her world became foreign to her without tight control. She leaned on them and it felt right.

The food arrived without much fanfare. Raquelle, who usual ate her fill and then some, pushed her food around her plate, making an attempt.

"Rape. I had no idea." The words fell from her lips.

"You were too young, but I knew something was off when you came back home. Papa ridiculed you for not being able to hack it. You closed yourself off from everyone for a while and reemerged as a full grown adult. You had supreme control over everything in your life. Then you decided to open the studio." Mara reflected.

"Yeah, it's funny what we use as a crutch. Do you know how hard it is to have that much control over everything? I thought if I reined everything in, I could control what happens to me. I guess the joke's on me because the last couple of days have been one upheaval after another." A nervous laugh escaped her with a shuddering breath.

"How did Dean take all this? You were with him when all this came out." Raquelle's curiosity piqued about Dean's reaction.

She laughed. "Turns out he's slaying his own dragons. There are some things from his past that haunt him. He hasn't gone into all of it yet. I'll wait for him to tell me. He was there when I needed him. That's a new one for me. No one has ever been there. No one has ever worried about my happiness. He makes me feel wanted. Just the way I am." She spread her arms out.

Mara found some levity in the conversation. "Hey, we never slay dragons. Dragons are our friends."

She had an attachment to her dragon Eros or rather Mac. She wouldn't give up either of them.

"I guess I can say you might need to see a therapist. I can recommend one." Mara grabbed her hand and squeezed as Raquelle put her hand on top of both of theirs.

They would always be there for each other through thick, thin, and everything in between.

The unbreakable bound held together by silkworm's thread.

Mara's eye got wide as she looked around. She could always sense Mac before she saw him. She and Raquelle followed her gaze. Down the street a large Scotsman charged toward them with Sean Knight in tow. People moved out of his way, unusual for New York City sidewalks. He didn't look happy.

"Oh, God, he looks pissed off," Raquelle muttered.

Mac came to a stop at the table, with hands on his hips. Bending down, he came face to face with Mara. "Is there a reason why your phone keeps going to voicemail after one ring? Could it be you don't have the friggin' thing turned on?" His mouth drew a tight line.

"Oh shit!" Mara scrambled into her purse, dragging out her cell phone. She had a habit of not turning it on when she left the apartment.

Mac snatched up a chair from another table and sat down. Sean did the same, sitting next to Leigha. "If there's an emergency, I can't reach you. You need to remember to turn your phone on." He pleaded with her.

"I know. I'm sorry. I was doing so well for a while." Her body shrank as her face fell.

"Well, we have an emergency. Your mother called me trying to find you. Thank God you told me where you were going today." His eyes cast in sadness.

"What's wrong? What's happened?" Raquelle panicked.

"Your father's been taken to the emergency

room. We need to get there as soon as possible. I got the company car to drive us down there." He held her hand. "Mara, it doesn't look good." He didn't try to hide his feelings. His face crumpled in sorrow.

CHAPTER 19

Leigha's blood rushed in her ears. One more thing out of her control. She cared for her father despite their turbulent relationship.

Mac herded everyone in the back of the suburban. They squeezed into the tight space. "Everyone, this is Sean Knight. He's my boss at MBK. I think you've met him once before."

Heads nodded in acknowledgement, mumbling a 'Hi' as the news of their father left everyone dazed.

She looked over. Sean wore a tight smile. His eyes focused on her.

He leaned in closer. "I'm sorry for the intrusion. Mac and I were headed to check out a lead on another case when he got the call. If there's anything I can do for you, let me know." His eyes were sincere, but she wondered about his heart. Word had it he was a player. He went through women like water. He grabbed her hand, holding it momentarily. His contact gave her little comfort while she worried about the condition of her father.

The car ride to the hospital remained cloaked

in nervous silence. Outside things rushed by, beeping, clanking, and carrying on. The world inside slowed, suspending them in anticipation.

Everyone rushed out of the car, charging into the emergency room. Reality assaulted them, with crying babies, grimaced faces, and an overbearing antiseptic smell.

Mara rushed to the desk with her and Raquelle on each side. "Where can we find Antonio Luccenzo?"

Without looking up, the nurse dryly asked, "Are you family?"

"Yes. We're his daughters."

"Fine. You can go see him. Room 5 at the end of the hall." Her eyes lacked even a sliver of sympathy amidst the chaos.

Mara turned to Mac and fell into his arms. He stroked her back, whispering reassuring words in her ear. She ached to have what they had. The battle within her raged on between the need to lean on someone and being strong enough to handle everything on her own. Her thoughts wandered to Dean. She could use his strength right about now.

An arm wound around her waist snapping out of her internal dialogue. "I'll be here if you need anything, anything at all." Sean's eyes hazed with sadness.

She could easily anchor herself to his strength and warmth of his body, but she questioned his sincerity. Instead, she pulled away from him. "Thank you. I'll let you know."

She turned and grabbed her sisters' arms, leading them to the unknown. They maneuvered around gurneys and wheelchairs, stopping outside the curtain for room 5. Bracing herself, she pulled the curtain back, startled at the scene before her.

Agony painted Mama's face. Tears streamed down her cheeks. The word *bellas* left her lips on a whisper. She moved toward them in slow motion, hunched over as if it took all her energy to get to them. They formed a circle around her, embracing her as heartache seeped into them.

She peered over her mama's shoulder at a father she didn't recognize. His normally healthy olive skin was washed in ash. His body sank into itself. The machines around him beeped with life. A breathing tube was secured under his nose. How had this happened so quickly? She wanted answers.

When they were together as a family they mostly spoke Italian. "Mama, what happened?"

Her mama, Guilianna, looked ravaged by her emotions. "He got the flu but wasn't getting any better. Instead, he's got worse. I didn't know what to do, so I brought him here. I don't know what I'll do if he leaves me. He finally decided to retire and stay at home. He would still work in the studio but without all the travel and now this." She cradled her head in her hands. Sobs racked her body.

They stood there, holding each other in prayer. The doctor walked in to give them an update. "I'm afraid I don't have good news. His condition is worsening and there isn't much more we can do. He isn't responding to the antibiotics. Unfortunately, it's just a matter of time at this point. I wish I had better news for you. I'm sorry." Dr. Cherighini used his practiced sympathy face then hurried out through the curtain.

The four of them stood silently, staring at his motionless body in disbelief. His eyes were closed. The only sign of life was the slight up and down motion of his chest followed by the beeping machine.

He half opened his eyes. "Guilianna, are my girls here?" His clear blue eyes were now clouded with sickness as he wheezed.

Leigha stepped over to his bedside, holding his hand. Her vision blurred through teary eyes. "We're all here, Papa."

"I need to tell you something before it's too late." He coughed.

Her voice broke on a rasp. "Don't say that. Don't go."

"I tried to protect you from him the only way I knew how. He will come for you. Beware. He's dangerous."

Another coughing fit interrupted his warning. She dropped his hand and stood back, puzzled and shocked by his words. He wasn't making any sense.

Mara and Raquelle came to the side of the bed to help him sit up until the coughing subsided.

His eyes traveled to each of them. "I did what I had to do to protect you. If I stayed away then their eyes would be on me and not you. I missed so much all these years. I missed you terribly. I stayed away out of love for you. I will always love you." A single tear escaped his eye, traveling down his cheek. Regret and despair shone in his eyes.

She had never seen her father cry. In that moment, something broke in her. Had she ever really known him? Why was he showing himself now?

He closed his eyes, exhausted from his life-altering speech. She stood, watching him, waiting for him to open his eyes and continue. But he didn't. He slipped into unconsciousness, pulling his cryptic message with him.

The three of them turned to Mama as recognition flashed in her eyes. A small smile formed on her lips and then faded. She hung her head down, avoiding their gazes and questions.

"Mama, what's he talking about? None of this makes sense." Something gnawed her. Was he being delusional?

She looked up at her daughters. Intensity filled her eyes. "Later." She nodded her chin in the direction of her husband. "We need to be with him right now." Getting up slowly, she made her way over to the bed. She put her arm around Raquelle, who sobbed into her shoulder as she held her husband's hand.

Grief filled the room as he took his final breath. The beeps became a continuous sound. Life had stopped yet the noise went on. His spirit left his body behind along with four broken hearts. They came together to hold on to each other once more. Tears of sadness took precedence over the questions about his final message.

Mara broke away from the group. She hit one button on her phone. "I need you," she said just above a whisper through broken words.

Seconds later, a scuffling could be heard down the hallway. Mac struggled with hospital staff, making his way to Mara.

"Get the fuck out of my way. She needs me." His voice bellowed in the hall as people mumbled around him.

He shoved the curtain aside and encased a broken Mara in his arms. He was always a breath away. Nurses followed him in, unhooking their father's lifeless body from the monotone machines. Numbness took over Leigha's body.

Sean came to her side. "Are you okay?"

"I don't want to talk about it." She wrapped herself in her arms putting her head down. He closed in about to hold her when turbulent air whipped away from her.

"Get your friggin' hands off of her," Dean growled.

"I didn't know she belonged to you, Dean," Sean hissed through his teeth but knew he'd been beaten.

He got nose to nose with Sean. "Well, she does. So back off, mate."

"I'm sorry for your loss." Sean pulled his jacket together by the lapels and left.

In her maze of feelings, clarity about this man hit her full-on. He came to comfort her.

He didn't need words. He wrapped her in his arms, rocking her slowly. She whimpered softly, letting her emotions go, the pain, control, questions, and nightmares. Hearing the heartbreak of her sisters' weeping clawed at her. She connected with them more than ever. Their mama would need them more than ever before. She gave Mac a slight smile as a thank you for calling Dean. He nodded his head in return.

Mac broke the muffled blanket of grief. "This

may not be the best time, but I need to talk to you. Something's not sitting right with me about your father. I think you need to order a tox screen and check for anything unusual."

She guessed what he wasn't saying. Their father may have been poisoned. She shuddered at the thought. Who would poison an artist? Did all of this have anything to do with his ominous message?

She broke in. "If you think that is best then we will request a tox screen." She wanted to head off her sisters and Mama from any questions. No one's thoughts were clear at this point.

Mara turned to the group. "We're going home with Mama tonight. I don't want her to be alone. Besides, we have a funeral to plan."

It amazed her how well Mara handled Papa's death. Raquelle, on the other hand, was a mess, gripping onto Mama like a life raft.

Dean held her hand. "Let's get you out of here, eh? Your tea cup runneth over at this point." He kissed her forehead. His tenderness and strength made her want to crumble again.

They said their goodbyes and made their way out of the hospital. Her heart had lost a piece, but Dean was starting to fill it in. She could count on him. But she would be the tie that bound her sisters and Mama together for the next couple of weeks. The pillar couldn't crumble yet.

CHAPTER 20

A haze clouded the next couple of days. Between planning for a funeral, dealing with spiraling emotions and unanswered questions, Leigha lacked any emotional output. The four of them ebbed and flowed from one another, each of them aware of others' mixed emotions about Papa's death.

Her childhood bedroom brought up so many emotions. She grieved for a father who had shunned her as a person and an artist. Yet, the words on his deathbed didn't match that man. He spoke of protection and the regret at not being more a part of their lives. It seemed he was forced to be someone he didn't want to be.

The overwhelming realization of the source of her nightmares couldn't be dealt with, casting her into another turbulent sea. She lapsed into the role of the pillar of strength for her sisters and mama, staying in her comfort zone. But like a wool shirt that went through the dryer, her control didn't fit anymore. She wanted to hand all over to someone else.

The knock on the door was followed by Mara's

head peeking around the corner. "Can I come in?"

She sat up, leaning on her forearm. "Of course."

"There you are." Raquelle pushed the door wide open and let herself in.

Mara and Raquelle sat on the foot of the bed in silence.

"Well?" Raquelle broke the tension with sarcasm.

"Well, what?" Mara's brows furrowed.

"Isn't anyone going to ask the question we're all thinking? What the hell was Papa talking about? Protecting us, he missed us and loved us. What the fuck?" Raquelle's face became bright red.

She sat up. "What are you so angry about?"

"What am I so angry about?" Tears bloomed at the bottom of her clear eyes. Her bottom lip trembled. "I'm angry at a father who was a stranger to me. For most of my life, he traveled coming home on rare occasions, leaving me to deal with his right-hand man. He was a ghost. Mama announces at his deathbed he was retiring and coming home for good. Now he's dead. I'll never get to know him. I'll never be able to share anything with him. Yet, given that, I'm so completely empty without him. There's a part of me that will never be filled. So, yeah, I'm pissed off." She swiped at her tears.

She recognized her anger and hurt.

Mara looked at her in anticipation. She moved around on the bed, picking at the thread in the quilt. "At least you weren't the thorn in his side. I could do nothing right." She laughed nervously. "I'm dealing with this in therapy. My relationship with him affected all my choices in life. His final words caught me off guard too. Because he loved us so much, he stayed away to protect us, doesn't make him a saint. I'm confused. What do his words really mean?"

Leigha sagged against her pillow. "He's even more of a mystery to me. Who's coming after me? I have no idea who 'he' is. Papa shunned me from as young as I can remember. Mama hovered over me like she was protecting me from something. I have a lot of questions for her I want answers to." Curiosity churned in her gut like bitter bile rising to the surface. She couldn't grieve for a relationship that had never formed.

"Like there wasn't enough mystery and drama in Cancun. We had to bring the drama home with us." Raquelle blew out an exasperated breath.

"And what about the tox screen Mac wants done? I didn't ask him why. I don't think I want to know." Sometimes denial worked well for Mara.

She wore her CSI cap again. "I think Mac's looking for poison in Papa's body."

"I can think of a few people who would want to poison him. He wasn't the easiest person to work for from what I understand." She and Mara stared at Raquelle with their mouths gaping open.

"How did you come across this information?" Another twist to the mystery.

"Let's just say an inside source and leave it at that. It's bedtime for Bonzo, girls. Ciao." Raquelle gave them each a hug before she left for her room.

"I'm more confused than ever by all of this. What do you think is going on? You seem to have some insight to all this investigative stuff." Mara always looked to her for answers.

"I can honestly say I know nothing. It's more of a mystery than I care to admit."

"And what about Dean?" Mara's finger poked her.

"I can't even think straight. I'll deal with him later."

"Oh, is that what you think? He's called you every day wanting to check in on you. I've been sneaking Mac in at night. He wants to be with me through this. I couldn't keep him away even if I wanted to. He's always there. I can't do this without him. Let Dean in." Mara's eyes pleaded with her.

"Why have you been sneaking him in? You're a grown woman." She ignored Mara's demand.

"Really? And how do you think Mama would be with me sleeping with a man under her roof?" Mara smiled for the first time in days.

"Good point. We better get some sleep. Tomorrow is going to be a long day with the funeral." Mixed emotions consumed her. She hated to admit it. She needed Dean.

They hugged good night and Mara left to be with her rock.

She lay awake, listening to the winter winds making an entrance, leaving fall behind. A shiver ran through her, not knowing what her future held or the outcome. Her lace of control became thinner as time ticked on out of her favor.

CHAPTER 21

Windshield wipers slapped away the heavy rain as he followed the winding driveway up to the house. Perched at the top of the hill stood the manor shrouded in inky blackness. He knew the backdoor would be open for him. The overwhelming need to protect her took over. He made a phone call to the one person he knew would help him.

He got out of the car, threw his hood over his head, and made a run for the backdoor. The handle clicked open without effort. According to the directions he would use the back staircase to access her room. He brought his pick set in case she locked her bedroom door at night.

He slipped up the stairs crouched low, grabbed the door handle, and let himself into her room. Even with the room cast in darkness, he could make out her shape. She breathed too hard to be asleep. An expert in stealth, eagerness took over with desire in his sights.

He gingerly put his hand on her shoulder. As she turned over to scream, his hand covered her mouth.

"Shh, it's me." Dean looked in her horrified eyes.

"Oh my God. You scared the shit out of me. What are you doing here?" she said through labored breaths.

"You've been avoiding me. You should know by now, I won't be ignored. There's a lot going on between us and I need to see where we end up. Don't shut me out now, babe." He held her by her shoulders with determination.

"I can't deal with you right now. You need to go before someone finds out. By the way, who let you—Mara. What a little sneak. She's been hanging around with Mac too long."

"Can't or won't? Doesn't matter to me." His fingertips brushed the stray hairs from her forehead. "I want to be here for you. You're going through a lot. Let me be the person you can lean on. You can count on me. Mac shared what your father said before he died. I imagine you're scared shitless. God knows it has something to do with everything that's been happening lately. I won't let anything happen to you." His mouth covered hers in a gentle kiss. Her sweet crisp taste made him want to fold himself in her softness.

She kissed him back with hunger. Her tongue pushed into his mouth, looking for a playmate.

"Ah, ah, ah, not so fast. Have you ever asked yourself why you escape through sex? I won't let you bury yourself in me. Although, I would like to bury myself in you, someday." He stroked her cheek.

She smiled through glassy eyes. "Now that you mention it, it all seems to be coming together now that I know the truth. How do you know so much about the human condition especially when it comes to me?"

"I survived war and PTSD. You have to feel it to get to through it. It's the way life works. Burying your emotions just leads to other things you may not get out from under." He stripped off his clothes down to his briefs. He lifted up the sheets and curled in behind her, molding her body to him. Her warmth brought him peace, at least for a while.

She finally let go as a deluge of tears came without warning.

"Let it out, babe."

"Mama." She gulped down a breath. "She has so much on her plate between Papa's death and his mysterious final words. I think she's carrying a burden of knowing what's behind his words. I ache for her. Tomorrow's going to be torture."

"And what about you? Are you ready for tomorrow? You seem to take care of others before yourself."

"I'll get through like I always do."

"I wish you didn't feel the need to. You need to get some sleep so you can be ready for tomorrow." He rocked her to sleep, stroking her arms and legs. Her breath evened out and she fell asleep within minutes.

He skipped the fact they were already running a detailed background check on her father and mother.

CHAPTER 22

The rain beat on the window. Huddling under the covers didn't keep out the cold. He had left to avoid detection. Leigha's mind fogged up. Her body ached from emotional exhaustion. She wanted nothing more than to lock the door to shut out the world. The funeral would bring artists from all over the world to pay their respects. The fake smiles would cover up thoughts of good riddance. They came to celebrate the death of their competitor, hoping to be the next shining star. The art world was nothing if not competitive. Artists lived for their creativity to gain notoriety. In the end, the work paled to the importance of the money.

Her papa's words came back to her. He would always say, "These new artists know nothing of classic art. People pay more for what they imagine they see rather than what's really there." His philosophy reflected the times.

The thought brought a smile. Her tender thoughts of him were few and far between. She knew very little of him and understood even less. Their relationship ended disconnected. But there were snippets she held on to like a favorite snapshot.

She stretched her legs and sat on the side of the bed. Dread came over her as she thought about the day ahead. The face she would have to create to greet the admirers and haters alike made her stomach turn.

It took every ounce of energy to make it down to the kitchen. She would have to dig deep to make it through the rest of the day. The kitchen resembled a roomful of zombies pushing food around on their plates. Their eyes focused on nothing. The scent of coffee permeated the air. Mama always made coffee using a French Press. She said it was the purest form and best tasting coffee. When it came to food and drink, Mama was rarely wrong.

Mara stared at her cup as she said, "Good morning. Did you have a good night with Dean?" She raised her brows and smirked, enjoying the dig.

"Yes." Her body stiffened as she glanced over at Mama.

"And Marabella, did you have a good night with Mac?" Mama smiled, winking at her.

Mara gasped. "How did you know? He's so quiet it's frightening sometimes."

"Do you think I don't know what goes on under my own roof? Besides, the two of you weren't exactly quiet about it." Mama put her hands on her hips as Raquelle roared with laughter.

Laughter burst the bubble of dread as tears formed in their eyes. Mama came over to hug each of her girls. She whispered the words "*i miei bambini*" as she kissed them each on the forehead. "We will get through today together. We've survived together this long."

The sisters nodded in agreement. They made their way back to their rooms to prepare to say goodbye in their own very different ways.

Mac and Dean arrived ahead of the limo to escort them to the funeral home. She went to hug Dean. "You don't give up, do you?"

"Not on your life. I'm here for as long as you want me." He hugged her fiercely as she willed herself not to cry.

She leaned back. "Did you just sniff my hair?"

"Yes. As a matter of fact, I did. I needed my fix. I like the smell of gardenias on you. It's my connection to home." Sadness covered his eyes like heavy curtains.

"I'm sorry. By all means, sniff away." She held his face in her hands.

He wiggled under her skin like no one else ever had before. Her chest tingled. She liked the idea she reminded him of home. She didn't know what she would do if she couldn't go back to her home, her family.

Unbearable silence filled the car ride to the funeral home. Rigid bodies held together by emotions that hovered under the surface of thin ice. They all held hands to brace themselves for what was to come.

She could see the line that had started to form at the entrance to the funeral home. The top of a large white tent appeared in the background. It would serve as an overflow to the cramped space of the reception area.

Upon arriving, the director ushered them to the back room for a private moment before their papa was displayed to the rest of the world. The casket lay open toward the back of a dark paneled room with deep red carpet. No brightness lit the area.

"I will go say my goodbyes." Mama kissed each of her daughters on both cheeks and made her way to the empty shell that awaited her.

Mara and Raquelle sat down as she quietly made her way closer to the scene about to unfold.

"*La mia bella marito.*" Mama always called him my beautiful husband. "What a mess you left behind. How do I explain anything to your *bambini*? You've left too soon. We still had more time together. We lost so much. Now I will never get you back. I'll pretend you are on a long business trip. I love you always. I will find you on the other side, *il mio amore.*"

She watched her mama hold his cold, lifeless hand, stroking his plastic-like face. Her heart splintered at the sight. Her mama found the love of her life and had to say goodbye way too soon. She turned back to her sisters, watching their faces crumple in misery.

Mara went next to say her peace. She never touched him, talking in a soft voice not to be overheard. Raquelle came up behind her, holding her by the shoulders. Her emotions were a mixed bag of anger and grief. Her body shook from head to toe. Mara held her to her shoulder to try and calm her down.

After witnessing her sisters' torment, she found anger upstaged any grief. She made her way to the casket, leaning on the side, her hands balled in fists. "Why? Why didn't you want me? Was I so terrible? You pushed me away at every turn. Do you think I wasn't creative enough? Well, newsflash, plenty of people find my photography creative and beautiful. I looked to my family on the road for support and where did that get me? I got raped." Her arms shook. Emotions took over. With each word, her voice became stronger and louder. "You were never there for me. You never wanted me. Then you leave me with this goddamn cryptic message. What the hell am I supposed to do with that? Who is he? Who's coming for me?" Her curled hands reached out to him. She stopped short of his neck. So startled at her actions and words, she jumped back from the casket. The last bind holding her together ripped loose with no hope of repair. She held her head in her hands, sobbing uncontrollably. Her body shook and pain threaded her muscles. All these years, she repressed the memory because she blamed her father. How could she blame him for something that wasn't his fault? Because he should have been there all along. Instead, she had to stand on her own through everything, burying her true self in order to survive, creating her armor of strength.

Their arms captured her from behind. Murmured Italian words surrounded her with love and reassurance. They didn't understand her crumbling walls. Like a butterfly, she curled up in her chrysalis, waiting to spread her wings and fly. She could hear her mama asking her sisters what was wrong and commenting she had never seen her like this. They gave the excuse that the break-ins had been too much and this was her outlet.

Mama didn't know about the rape. She wasn't sure she wanted to share it with her.

She reached to her familiar place of control to pull herself together as her only option. They went to the reception area to greet the guests, who'd flown in from the four corners of the world to give their sympathy. The crowd ran the gamut from aunts, uncles, cousins, artists, agents, and gallery owners.

She stood between Mara and Raquelle in birth order.

"Bernardo, thank you for coming," Mama falsely chirped as he kissed her on both cheeks.

Raquelle's body went rigid. She stared straight ahead at the sound of his name.

"What's wrong?" She leaned into Raquelle's ear.

Raquelle's eyes widened. "Nothing."

Bernardo gave his condolences to Mara and then to her. As he approached Raquelle, his hands balled into fists and then released.

"Bella, I'm so sorry for your loss. But you remain as beautiful and talented as ever." A sneer crossed his face.

Raquelle coolly offered her cheek. "Thank you." She pushed him away with hidden disgust. Her hands shook slightly.

"What's that about? I've never seen you back down from anyone," she whispered.

"It's nothing. Mind your business. You have enough on your plate." Raquelle looked coldly at her.

She would come back to that conversation someday.

She looked around and realized there were hundreds of millions of dollars standing in that room. An idea presented itself as a memorial for their father.

Hours later, as the crowd began to thin, they sat down with achy tired feet, worn out hands, and rosy cheeks. Mac and Dean joined them as they served as runners all day to keep them hydrated and fed.

"So I have an idea to honor Papa's memory. If all these people really loved him, then they can participate in Artists for the People charity. We create an online warehouse of artists' works. Each work sold donates one percent to a different charity such as domestic violence, child hunger, victims of sexual assault, autism, diabetes, and any others we want to add. We'll start with our own pieces first and let it grow. What do you think?"

Mara's eyes filled with tears. "I think it's a great idea." She put her hand over hers.

"Me too." Raquelle joined in on their three musketeers' handshake.

"Me three." Mama's hands covered theirs.

Smiles crossed their faces as his tragedy had turned into something to help other people. His mysterious message was put on hold at least for now.

CHAPTER 23

Uncomfortable silence veiled the ride back to her apartment. She slumped in the passenger's seat, resting her head on the window. The vacancy in her eyes came from the pain of loss, not grief. She had seen something she couldn't unsee. Lost in thought, Dean didn't disturb her with his words. He held her hand, lightly stroking her palm. She needed comfort not questions. Those could wait.

He parked the car on the street and helped her out. She leaned on him as he all but carried her to the elevators. Once they were in her apartment, his words pierced their silent bubble, startling her. "Do you want me to stay?"

She spun around with a tortured look on her face. "Of course. You never stopped being there for me. Not once. Not like him." Unable to finish her thought, he held her to him as she whimpered in his shoulder. His heart ached for her. He was all too familiar with an absentee father.

"Let's get you undressed and ready for much-needed sleep." He brushed her tears away from her cheeks, hoping tomorrow would bring some cheer to her shattered hazel eyes.

Her pale face accented the day's ravage to her soul. He stripped her out of her clothes, replacing them with an old cotton T-shirt from her drawer. She moved like a child having a parent ready them for bed. He got in bed, snugging her into the crook of his arm. Her head lay on his shoulder. She threw her leg over him with her arm across his shoulder making sure he couldn't escape.

"Do you want to talk about what happened when you said goodbye to your father? Something changed in your face when you came out." Her fingers instantly curled into his chest as her nails dug in. "Babe, under different circumstances, I might be into a little pain. This isn't one of those moments."

"Oh. I'm sorry. I wasn't paying attention." She looked up and loosened her grip on him. "What came out of me had nothing to do with grief and everything to do with anger. I'm angry with him for not being there for me, shunning me, and excluding me from the family. I blamed him for my rape. How crazy is that?" Her face fell and then hardened. Her admission came without tears. She waited for his reaction.

He continued to stroke her in a gesture of comfort. "He made you turn to people who weren't family, forcing you to trust them. It's not crazy. It's difficult not being able to live up to a parent's expectation."

A spike drove into his chest as he thought about his own twisted relationship with his father. A father who hung him out to dry with all the wrong people. Another reason he couldn't go back to Australia. The burn came from the inside, scarring the same wound over and over.

In a small childlike voice, she said, "I'm Wilbur. I'm the pig he didn't want. Now I know why I bonded with the story as a child. He would've sent me to slaughter if he could. That's why his final words to me don't make any sense." She let out an exasperated breath.

He rolled her on her back, tracing her face with his fingers. "He may not have wanted you, but I do. I crave you all the time. It takes everything I have to hold back until you show me you're ready. So far, I like what I see."

She looked up at him with tired, soft eyes. Her hardness disappeared as she let go a little bit deeper.

He kissed her tenderly, sucking on her lips and invading her mouth with his tongue. That was enough. He wouldn't take advantage of an open wound. She needed to be healed and whole again before they would be ready for each other.

"You need some sleep." Without argument, she turned over, giving him her back as he cocooned her from behind.

Lost in his own thoughts, he watched her sleep peacefully. She had been through so much and yet she continued to grow and move forward. There were so many unanswered questions in her life. His skin prickled at the thought of the words her father said, "He will come for you." Who would come and what did he want? The uneasy feeling caught him off guard. He squeezed her tighter to him. Questions and connections spun in his head. He fell asleep in a restless slumber.

Light streamed in through the blinds, casting a

warm glow on the arm around her waist. Curled up tightly next to him like a cat in a fluffy bed, she purred, which made him chuckle. He'd place a bet she didn't know she snored.

He climbed out of bed and headed for the shower. Warm water rained down on him, washing away the rank smell of death. He washed with her gardenia shampoo to wipe away the mustiness. His thoughts traveled right back to her. Peacefulness came over him just to be with her. The touch of her skin, the challenge in her eyes, and perfect round, small tits had his cock hardening between his legs. It had been a while since he got laid mostly because no women had interested him. The woman lying in the other room had him rock hard and very interested. He could have easily gotten himself off. But he wanted to save it for her. He required all of her. He needed to stop his thoughts otherwise he'd have nothing left. His shifted his mind to his time in Afghanistan. That always deflated the beast.

He got out of the shower and wrapped a towel around him. He tiptoed into the bedroom and went in search of his change of clothes. There she lay looking like his wet dream. The sun shone behind her, making her glow. Her tousled hair gave her a wild look. She held the sheet up to cover her naked body. His body responded immediately as he tented the towel.

"Well, looks like someone is happy to see me this morning." She laughed, throwing her head back.

The freedom in her face made her shine from the inside. The young girl from the photos of her modeling days had returned. He moved like a panther toward its prey with one knee propped on the bed. Her smile faded, making him collapse on his calves.

"What's wrong?" he asked.

"Truth. How are you still here? God, I'm so fucked up. Look at what's happened over the last couple of weeks. Between the break-ins, being chased, my father dying leaving a mysterious message, you should be gone by now. If I were you I would run as far away as possible." The bright light shining in her eyes moments before left, shut down, replaced by the hurt child discarded by a parent who didn't love her.

"It's where I went wrong before. I left without any real thought to anyone else. My selfishness cost someone their life. I wasn't paying attention. I'm paying attention now." His eyes panned down to her chest. "Do your nipples always stand at attention for no reason?"

Her eye widened at his new confession about himself.

He trailed his thumb from her jaw, down her neck, between her breasts. "I'm not leaving this time. We'll get through this together. I want you so bad it hurts to look at you."

She shrugged away from him with a smile. "I don't think that's such a good idea. I wouldn't want to be just a distraction for you." She huffed out a breath. "I need you to be totally with me when we make love." She looked at him coyly with half a smirk, letting the sheet drop to her waist.

"Oh, is that the way you're going to play this?"

His towel dropped off him and onto the floor. He grabbed her by the upper arms and with a gravelly voice said, "By the time I'm done with you, you will be begging for more of my distraction and screaming my name."

He nibbled at her neck and heard her gasp.

"Tie me up."

He leaned back, startled by her request. "What?"

"I want to know what it feels like to give someone else control. Can you do that?" Determination set in her eyes.

"Hold on to the headboard and don't let go until I tell you to." He didn't need to tie her up. Too much, too soon.

Her hands trembled slightly as she held on tight. He put his hands over hers. His body completely covered hers. His cock settled between her legs.

He nibbled her ear. "I'm not leaving unless you throw me out. You better be damn sure this is what you want. We need to find each other and figure this mess out together. So the question is, do you want me to leave?"

She answered on a whimper, "No."

He leaned away from her, allowing the cool air to come between their heat. "I'm sorry, I didn't hear you."

She looked up at him. Hurt covered her eyes. "No. Don't leave me." Her eyes searched his for any doubts. "I've never said that to anyone."

"Oh, babe, that I'm sure of."

His mouth crashed down on hers as he tugged on her hair, but her hands never left the headboard. He released her. His heart beat faster in his chest. She arched her back, pushing into him, challenging him.

"Close your eyes and feel everything between us. No thinking allowed. Do you trust me to take care of you?" He swallowed the true meaning of his words, words he should have said years ago.

"Yes." Her eyes zeroed in on him without wavering.

He pushed her hair out of her face. He started with her long, slender neck, licking, biting, and kissing. Each time she let out a soft mew, his cock got harder. His fingertips skated down her arms, leaving a trail of goose bumps. His tongue teased the valley of her breasts, drawing small circles with his fingers as they caressed her bare mound. Already wet for him, he slid his middle finger along her folds. Her hips began to move back and forth.

His finger froze in place. "Stop moving. You don't control this."

"Please," she begged, out of breath.

He continued to tease her as his fingers slid into the seam of her ass. Her body went rigid. "So we're in some uncharted territory here." He bent down close to her ear. "We'll save that for another time." Shivers went through her.

His finger continued to work her with an in and out motion while she stayed stone-still. She clamped down, ready to come. He grabbed her vibrator from the drawer in the nightstand.

"No. I've played with toys enough lately." She peered over at him with determination in her eyes. "I want you inside me. For once, I want to know what it feels like to really be wanted by a man." Her eyes glistened with tears.

"Come here." He wiped a tear away from each eye. "Babe, I want you. All of you, including all your secrets, but never any lies or omissions."

"I don't need to lie to you. You're the keeper of my secrets."

"And you're the keeper of mine. Are you clean and on birth control?"

"Yes and yes."

"Good. Because I want to experience absolutely everything with you. I can't wait to light up those eyes." He kissed her tenderly at first and then devoured her mouth, neck, and shoulders. The wait was over.

CHAPTER 24

Leigha lay back as he hovered above her, showing his appreciation for her small, round breasts. Her mind and body floated on a high. They made their own chemistry, designed for them. She had never felt this way about anyone. He cared for and valued her. He took control from her by being there for her. His eyes showed her that he saw her soul, broken and controlling, yet he volunteered to get cut on her edges.

The soft moans coming from her had her biting her lip to stop them.

"Babe, let it go. Give it all to me."

She looked up at his clear ocean blue eyes. She could lose herself in them on a daily basis. His devastating smile added to his appeal. When she came out the other side of this, she didn't know who she would be.

The head of his cock nudged her entrance as he played with her.

"Don't you think I've waited long enough? You're such a tease."

"Maybe. But I'm worth the wait," he said smugly.

She threw her head back to laugh as he pushed in a little further. "You're so cocky."

"You have to be in our line of work otherwise you lose your edge." He nudged in a little further, emphasizing the word edge. "I think I see your edges softening."

Their understanding fused them. A moan came from deep within her. She wrapped her long legs around his waist, locking him in with her ankles.

Panting, he stilled inside her. "Look at me. It's never felt like this." He continued slowly. The tension in his face showed his restraint. He rubbed her clit with his thumb as she tightened.

The moment held so much intimacy, she wanted to turn away but couldn't. He was her truth. He brought out the best in her.

"You feel so good."

He kept his eyes locked on hers thrusting harder and faster. The spiral began at her clit, moving outward, claiming the rest of her body. She screamed his name as he filled her, coming right after her.

They panted in unison. Sweat covered their bodies, sticking them together. Her hard, confining lines fell away. She crossed another bridge to the woman she lost so long ago. She had never experienced such intensity with any of her past lovers. Her mind tried to catch up to the message her body sent her. Ablaze with new sensations, her body slowly attached itself to her newfound emotions.

He lay on top of her without his full weight. "If you think anymore, the steam is going to start rolling out of your ears." His voice muffled in the pillow next to her head.

He lifted his head. "And the light's shining in your eyes again, babe. Someone's going to have to make sure that happens often."

"I suppose you are just the man for the job." She squeezed his shoulder.

"I'm the only man for the job from now on." He gave her a crooked smile at his own big ego.

Her tone became serious. "That's the first time I've had an orgasm during sex. You being inside of me…I can't even begin to describe it other than chemical. Toys are great foreplay but could never take the place of the real thing."

"It's a lot more than chemical. And no one can ever take the place of me. So I guess you're not a lesbian?"

"Nope. I guess my experimental phase is over."

"Well, let's not get carried away. I have more experiments to try with you." He laughed.

Her veil of control slipped off dissipating as it hit the floor. Total control wasn't needed anymore. She found someone to take care of her when need be. His eyes danced with joy as he got up to get her a washcloth. His backside was something to behold.

She hugged the pillow, watching him fill the space of the room. He leaned down to clean her. She went to close her legs and scooted away. The gesture felt too intimate, that he would take the time to take care of her.

He leaned back with a frown. "What's wrong?"

"I'm not used to being cared for like this. You're a remarkable man, tough on the outside, soft on the inside."

"Hey, don't let that get out. I've got a reputation to maintain. You're an incredible woman. You better get used to it, 'cause there's a lot more where this came from. I take care of what's mine." He winked at her and continued to concentrate on the task at hand. "I want to make you breakfast and go for a ride. You interested?"

"Yeah, I'm interested." She laughed at her double entendre.

He pulled on his briefs and sauntered to the kitchen to serve up breakfast. She heard him clanking around as cabinet doors opened and closed. The energy in her lonely space came to life. He filled it with joy and happiness. He was a force to be reckoned with.

CHAPTER 25

Dean needed a distraction from the scene that unfolded before him. Cooking would give him an escape. His hands trembled. He had been here before. Last time, he had completely fucked it up. The fierce connection to the beautiful, strong creature in the next room would be his undoing. His past was catching up with him. Did he honestly think he could bury himself in work and one-night stands to keep him from facing his guilty mistakes? Every time he thought about not being able to save her, the winch tightened in his chest, cutting off his air.

Memories flooded him as he hunched over the cooking eggs. No other options presented themselves other than to keep Leigha safe. The emotions pulled at him from several directions, demanding his attention. Over the years he had tried to hammer them down, hoping they would leave of their own accord. He had even tried to drink them away without success.

"Hey, you okay?" She blew into the room like a warm Australian ocean breeze. They already had connections that only true lovers have with each other. That link that allowed you to feel and sense things about the other person.

He turned around and pasted on his model smile. "Yeah, just remembering something."

She walked over next to him. Her eyes read his lie. "The model smile doesn't work on me and the eggs are going to burn."

She lifted the pan off the flame, rescuing them from an inferno. This woman would either break him or rescue him from his depths of hell.

As he pulled her to him, a foreboding chill skated under his skin. He shoved it to the back of his mind and let it go. No words were needed. She hugged him back with the same intensity. He nuzzled her neck, feeling her heartbeat. He didn't want to let her go, ever.

When she leaned back, her eyes said everything was going to be okay. "Let's eat and go for a ride." The control had momentarily shifted back to her. He thanked God for her strength and ability to handle him in any emotional situation.

She pulled the plates and cups from the cupboard, turned around, and froze. Her smile spread from ear to ear. "What's that?"

"It's Babe." He had second thoughts about his gift.

"I love it. The tail is the handle. It's so small."

"It's made for tea not coffee. Promise me you won't smash it to bits."

She laughed, reaching for the pink piglet teacup.

"Look at the bottom."

She turned over the cup where he had drawn a heart and written Fern. He loved seeing the light in her eyes.

"I'll take it everywhere I go and you'll be there too. Thank you. This is a treasure." She hugged it to her and kissed him softly.

She sat down, holding her cup. He plopped down in the chair at the table. His emotions felt like resistance bands pulling on his soul. One minute he waded in the shallow end, the next, dove in the deep end.

"By the way, why did Mac want all of our phones?" She never missed a thing.

"You now all have trackers on your phones so he can find you if need be. With everything going on, he didn't want to take any chances." He pushed his food around the plate. His emotions broke free running through his body recklessly.

"You have a secret. Care to share?" Her lips sealed the fork with egg on it.

He looked down at his plate. "Oh, babe, I have many secrets. Some I might need to share. Some I don't know if I can ever share." His life played like a double-edged sword. He lived one life while struggling to reach for another.

"I need some time," he begged her.

She nodded. Her eyes remained sad, but she didn't say anything else about it. They cleaned up the kitchen in silence and got ready for the ride.

The unusually warm day for October had them dress in jeans, leather jackets, and helmets. They took off on one of the dragon bikes. She got on the back, securing her arms around him. He loved the feel of her wrapped around him. This time her body relaxed into the ride.

The long ride out to the very end of Long Island would give him enough time to calm his internal motor. How he got so tangled, he hadn't a clue. He didn't want to think about the only other woman who had gotten to him like this. Leigha wasn't her. She had proven to be stronger and seemed to be dealing with her current discovery of past trauma. His thoughts wandered. His body became rigid with guilt. Her hand left around his waist stroked his thigh with comfort and understanding. He held her hand to let her know he got her message.

The ride didn't have the usual summer traffic. They passed old New England homes covered in ivy, draped in the colors of fall leaves. The air held a crisp warning of impeding winter, but they would make the most of the day.

They stopped to take a look at the lighthouse at the end of the peninsula then rode south to find a quiet spot. He parked the bike and took a blanket out of one of the saddlebags.

"When did you stash a blanket in there?" She stood back, arms crossed as he moved toward her.

He grabbed her hand, dragging her behind him. "After our first beach trip, I wanted to be prepared for our second." The sun warmed his face.

"Well, aren't you a little overconfident. After our last trip, I wouldn't have thought there would be another one." She jogged to stay up with him.

"Oh, you were in my sights from the first time I saw you. You are more or less like trying to catch a jaguar. Feisty as hell." He gave her a sideways glance.

He spread the blanket out on the grainy sand and sat down. He opened his jacket, patting the space between his legs. She smiled as she sat down.

His big arms hugged her in tight. He wanted to tell her so much but he would have to dig deep. He didn't want his nerves to prevent him from moving forward.

They sat in silence, letting the sound of the small crests of waves caress them. The need to protect her and keep her safe overwhelmed him. He sighed deeply. Being near the ocean always relieved tension for him. She seemed to be his new anchor, a reason to stay, not wanting to rush back to Australia.

As if she read his mind, she said, "We always end up near the ocean. It seems to be your go-to place. The place where you find inner peace."

"The ocean is the one place I find peace. I spent my childhood on the beach and in the ocean. It's where I'm most comfortable." His eyes became unfocused as childhood memories filled his head.

She leaned back to look at him. "You said you couldn't go back. Why?"

"It's a long story and one of my secrets." He pulled her back into him in a plea not to let that be the reason she wouldn't want him.

"Don't worry. I've got time. You were there for me. I can be there for you." The breeze blew her hair around her face, making her look like a mermaid.

It was his turn to ante up. Telling her might relieve some of the pressure. "First, you need to know what I'm about to tell you can't be repeated."

She nodded her head in acknowledgment.

"I guess I should start at the beginning." He stopped to look out over the ocean, holding back the pain of a pierced heart. "I grew up as a military brat, moving from place to place around the world. We never really got roots anywhere until I turned fourteen and we came back to Australia for good." He swallowed hard at his first memory of her as they entered the school together. But that story would never be told.

"In the tradition of the Wagner family, I entered the military at eighteen. God knows that was a mistake on so many levels." He laced his fingers over hers trying to rein in his emotions. "I worked my way up, becoming part of the ASIO, which is comparable to the FBI. My ever-loving father, Nick, is the director or dictator, whichever way the wind is blowing." Bile caught in his throat at the thought of the man he didn't recognize as his father anymore.

"Two years ago, I had a mission go south. I won't go into the details. Let's just say it put a bounty on my head, preventing me from returning to Australia. Oh, and the best part, as I came to find out, my father put it there, son of a bitch that he is." He hesitated, not sure he could continue.

The emotions he held down deep bubbled to the surface. The betrayal weighed heavily on him. He brought one arm up to hug around her shoulder, pulling her tightly to him.

His mouth skimmed her ear. "The worst part is what I left behind, my mother and my two sisters, Seraphina and Una. I have no contact with them. It would be too dangerous. He told them I'm deep undercover." He gritted the words out through his teeth. His breath hitched, aware he had never shared this part of himself with anyone. "So you see, I know something about sisters. I would protect mine with my life. I'm the oldest, but Seraphina is the one who got me into modeling. She still models. I catch her in print ads every now and then."

One of his tears slid down her cheek. She turned around, wrapping her legs around his waist. Her thumbs wiped his tear-stained face.

"The birds on your shoulders..." Her words were gentle and compassionate.

"Yea. I carry them with me always." The only words he could muster without breaking apart.

"I can't imagine what it would be like not to be able to see or contact my sisters. I would be devastated."

She kissed his face tenderly, eventually landing on his lips. He needed this moment of vulnerability. After all she had been through she still had room in her heart for him. She was the keeper of one of his secrets. He didn't think he would be strong enough to reveal the other one.

CHAPTER 26

Dean showed her the softest part of himself. He revealed the betrayal of a parent that cut him like dead weight from the rest of his family. Going to the ocean gave him that unbreakable connection to them. It brought back fond memories that he could hold onto for a moment until they disappeared like spray off a wave.

She didn't talk to him on the ride back to the city. He was cashed out with nothing left to give. He stayed focused on the road, holding her hand and stroking her fingers more for his reassurance that hers. She grounded him. His ship drifted without any land in sight until her strength gave him something to hold onto. His life resembled a hurricane, tossing him from end to end. She was the eye of the storm.

He took her back to his place, parking the bike in the garage. She got off the bike, took off her helmet, and held out her hand to him without saying a word. Some women were yappy, wanting to know more than you were willing to share. But not this one. She had a sixth sense for what he needed in turbulent times. He took her hand, leading them to the elevators. She placed her arms around his waist and looked up at him with a smile on her face.

He looked straight ahead and whispered, "I don't deserve you. I have too many demons."

"That's where you're wrong. Everyone deserves someone. Everyone has some form of darkness. You needed to find your matching piece. I guess you're stuck with me until this case is solved or you move back to Australia." She looked away.

He whispered, "Maybe I found a reason not to go back to Australia." He kissed the top of her head.

She squeezed him tighter without a word.

He opened the door to a space he hadn't seen in a couple of days. The mustiness greeted them head-on.

"I'm sorry. I didn't know you lived with your… grandmother?" Her tight lips curled at the ends, trying hide the humor in the plastic-wrapped furniture.

"Damn it. I need to get this remodeled. My grandmother gave me the apartment. I haven't completely redecorated it yet. Maybe you can help." He tried to give her half a smile, his only attempt for the day. "Why don't you go wash up while I make us dinner. On second thought, maybe not, you still smell like me and I like that."

He never brought women home. The escape was easier leaving the woman's place. But she belonged here with him. Her energy wrapped around him like a heavy cotton blanket, listening to his story without pity. She was there just for him. That was what he needed more than anything.

He pushed her against the front door and kissed her, needing to feel her. Piece by piece, he peeled her out of her clothes. She stood panting and naked before him. Her pale skin tinted pink against the large dark wooden door. Her hair mussed and her face glowed.

"You're such a goddamn beauty. You take my breath away." He stood back from her shirtless with hands hanging off his belt buckle. She had managed to pull off his shirt. His girl gave as good as she got.

The smile of a vixen lit up her eyes. "I can think of another way to take your breath away."

She sauntered over to him using her best runway walk and dropped gracefully to her knees. The connection between them deepened as their eyes locked. She would surrender to him when necessary but take control when he needed her to.

She moved her palm up and down the outside of his jeans, covering it with her mouth. Her hot breath made his cock harder.

"Jesus, babe." He started to unbuckle his pants.

She grabbed his hands and wiggled her finger back and forth. "Uh, uh, uh. You're not in control."

She finished the job he started, pulling down his jeans, not expecting him to be without underwear. "Nice. I guess someone expected to get lucky today." She smiled at him, licking her lips.

"You're going to be the death of me, angel." He went to grab his cock.

"Hey, no touching. That belongs to me. You just need to enjoy the ride."

She licked his well-endowed crown several times before letting it slide to the back of her throat. He let out a grunt of appreciation as he grabbed her hair, pulling it to one side. He didn't want to miss the show. She gazed up at him. He began to move his cock in and out of her mouth. With a pop, she let him hang in midair.

"Stop or I'll stop and forbid you to finish."

He threw his head back in laughter. "That's my girl."

She continued her assault by stroking his balls with her nails from underneath while slowly moving his cock in and out of her mouth. Her teeth teased. He hissed his pleasure. She quickened her pace. His balls tighten. She slowed and grabbed him at his base. He gritted his teeth, waiting for the agony of bliss. No direction was necessary. She knew what she was doing. He stroked her cheek, admiring the goddess at his feet. This time she would give him what he wanted and then some. She held him at the base while moving her mouth. Her lips tightened around him all while continuing to stroke his balls. When they tightened, she pressed her finger behind them. She held him in her mouth. He exploded in her as his warm essence slid down her throat. Every expletive flowed from his mouth until the final word, his favorite, 'Leigha.' She let his semi-hard cock slip from her mouth. She stood up, pressing her naked body to his.

He grabbed her ass and pulled her to him. "Babe, where did you learn that trick?"

"Truth?" Her lips were plump and red.

"Always."

Her shy eyes looked away from him. "I read about it in a book. I read. A lot."

"First the hand job and now this. My woman is full of surprises, and for God's sake, don't stop reading. I hear it's good for you." His racing heart hadn't calmed down.

She kissed him, biting his lower lip, and walked away. "I'm going to take a shower." She left him standing there with his pants down around his ankles, which summed up what she did to him every time.

CHAPTER 27

Leigha found the bathroom at the end of the hall. He knew how to decorate because the bathroom looked like a photo out of Architectural Digest. White marble double sink with various shades of blue tile was reminiscent of the ocean he grew up near. This was his homeland connection.

The rain shower trickled water down over her body. But her thoughts stayed with him. She never enjoyed giving blowjobs until now. A new feeling came over her. She wanted to please him, giving him a small escape from his torment. On more than one occasion he referred to her as 'his' and 'mine.' Her emotions twisted up inside. Her edges sharpened. The connection between them seemed so intense and held so much strength. It scared the crap out of her. She wasn't sure she was cut out for the long haul. He had never wavered in his conviction to be there for her. She could count on him no matter what. He was strong enough to bear her weight and then some. But she wondered at what cost. He carried so much already.

She got out of the shower, dried off, and wrapped herself in one of the blue fluffy robes hanging on the back door. There didn't appear to be remnants from any former lovers. But she didn't snoop around long enough to find out. She didn't want to know the answer. The robe hung on her and smelled like him, fresh and clean, making her heart sing.

She made her way back to the kitchen. The aroma of pasta made her salivate. "Someone knows what they're doing in the kitchen. It smells delicious."

The dining room table had been set for them. He appeared from the kitchen the way she had left him, shirtless.

"I hope you have a big appetite because I made a lot. I thought you might like red wine instead of whiskey tonight. I'll be having a Gold beer." His eyes moved down away from her.

He moved around the table as if he were going through the motions. He didn't make eye contact with her. His body stiffened, the complete opposite to the way he was before dinner. She began to fidget with her hands, not sure where she stood with him.

When he finally sat down, she watched as he pushed most of the food around, taking a bite every now and then. They played eye tag. She tried to catch his eye and he avoided hers. She began to eat to satisfy her hunger but then gave up, acquiescing to her nerves.

He ate with his left hand. His right hand balled in a fist next to his plate. She would give him his quiet time and space. She dropped her napkin on the table and got up to dress and leave.

"Sit down, Leigha."

He raised his head. His hooded eyes met hers as his mouth formed a taut line. His intensity crashed over her.

She sat down with hands clasped in her lap, waiting to take whatever he had to dish out. He would tell her they were over. He couldn't see her anymore. Wasn't this the way something this intense always ended? It would be best for both of them. She took a shallow breath, anticipating the snip of the tether. She would try and skate out of this unscathed.

"I want you." His face lacked expression, but his eyes glimmered.

"You just had me." Her brows cinched with confusion.

"No. I want you in my life for a very long time, as long as you will have me. I need you. I never thought I would need anyone. You're stronger than you even know. After I told you about my dysfunctional mess, you didn't even flitch. You can't deny our connection." His eyes softened a bit.

She read it as curiosity to her reaction after his proclamation. She was out of her element. This isn't what she could deal with right now.

"I think we need to slow down. There's a lot going on." The crack in her voice exposed her nerves. Her fingers twisted together.

He pushed his chair back and stalked toward her in nothing but jeans and bare feet. He scooted her back from the table and knelt in front of her. He pushed her robe to the side, exposing her long legs. She leaned back and gripped the arms of the chair.

"I've lost too much and I'm not willing to lose any more. Life burned a hole in me and you filled it. You understand and listen to me without judgment. We have something I'm holding on to. I've never felt this way. Not even…" He swallowed his words, bowing his head. His fingers gripped onto her thighs.

She sat there stick-straight like a cornered animal with nowhere to go. His words struck her. She tried to hold onto her little bit of control. The only words missing from his speech were 'I love you.' She was thankful they weren't said. She would be the one to decide what they became, but she couldn't deny the hold he had on her.

His head came up as his eyes locked onto her. "I know you're scared. I can see it in your eyes. I'll give you time. Just meet me halfway."

He got up and held out his hand. Without a word, she took his strong hand as the tether strengthened. He led her to the couch in the den without the plastic.

"Lie down, please."

Spooning seemed to be their thing as he lay down behind her. He stroked her and her eyes became heavy. He knew how to soothe her soul. She closed her eyes. The intensity of the moment coupled with a day of fresh air and confessions made her soul tired. Her last memory before sleep would be his tenderness.

CHAPTER 28

Leigha fell into a deep sleep on his oversize couch. Their arms and legs laced around each other. This had turned into their normal. He made her feel protected, wanted, and trusted. But did she trust herself enough to really be with him?

A fog had rolled in, making the outside look murky. The translucent curtain made her view out of focus and fuzzy. A chill pricked her skin, making her shiver. He was kidding himself if he thought this was real. She had too much on her plate. She didn't want to use him. Getting away and clearing her head was her only option.

She escaped his possessive hug without waking him. Memories of the conversation the night before ran like a loop through her head. He was so sure of himself and how he wanted them to be together. She needed time and space. Her inner peace came through running. She needed to sort through her emotions and find out where he fit in, if he fit in.

He slumbered peacefully. His dark lashes fanned out, giving him the look of a teenage boy. There were more secrets he held close. She could feel them below his surface. Something dark still haunted him. She wasn't sure she wanted to know what they were.

She got dressed in the clothes from the night before and headed out the door barefoot. Mission accomplished. She needed to screw her head on straight. The cage that confined and comforted her tightened more than ever. She couldn't shake it away. The risk was too great. The odds were against her after everything that had gone down. He wouldn't want her in the end. They would be a fling like she and Sydney. He would go on to find someone else. She would ride the wave until it hit the beach, tumbling like a fish out of water.

The fog wound through the streets like long fingers. People wore gloom like extras in a horror film. She couldn't shake her sense of impending doom. But she continued to run harder and faster than ever before. She hoped to outrun her encroaching feelings for him. She skipped over all the romantic songs as they came up on her iPod. Straight up hard rock for her.

At the end of the run, she convinced herself she was in complete control once again. He wouldn't weave his magic into her heart. They were too soon and too intense. Who had such intense feelings after knowing someone for a short time? What was undeniable was what they had shared in that time. She never opened up to anyone or felt as comfortable as she did with him. It shook her to her core. Yet he embraced all of her. Even as she exposed her abuse, he showed the tender side of himself. He shared a piece of himself with her. She wasn't sure what to do with it. She had always been the fixer of other people's problems. But he waded in and stayed there. She couldn't get a handle on any of it.

The fog off the river refused to lift, shrouding the buildings in blue gray mist, adding to her mood. She arrived at the studio around mid-morning but something felt off. Thoughts whirled in her head as she climbed the stairs. She slipped the key in the lock. The door opened without effort. Chloe must be inside already. She stepped in the eerily quiet studio to find a man with his back to her staring out the window. His shoulders sagged with his hands stuffed in his pockets.

"Excuse me?" Her voice shook.

The door closed behind her. The lock clicked in place. She turned around to two men in black suits. They stood with their hands folded in front of them, looking like something out of a gangster movie. Her anxiety spiked. She clutched her purse in front of her as if it were going to provide any kind of protection.

"Don't mind them. They are here for protection." His voice was confident and smooth. He folded his hands in front of him but made no move toward her.

The older gentleman was dressed in a custom-tailored, impeccable gray suit with blond hair and piercing hazel eyes. She couldn't identify his heavy accent. "Protection from what? Me? I'm sorry. I didn't get your name." She racked her memory in hopes of recalling him as a former client.

He turned to the men in black, giving them

instructions in a foreign language. She picked up on what she thought was Russian. Hair rose on her arms as the Russian connection flooded her mind, putting her on high alert. He walked to her as if he knew the place well. His eyes never left her face.

The men flanked the door and unbuttoned their jackets, revealing weapons underneath. She took a step back and stumbled. He reached out and caught her arm. She wrestled away from him. He stayed where he was, holding his hands up in surrender.

He put his hands down slowly, saying something to her in a language she didn't understand. His eyes glassed over. "My little angel," he repeated in English.

Her nerves came undone at the sight before her. Was this the him her father warned her about? She tried to mask her fear. "How can I help you?" Her soft voice didn't carry far in the empty space.

He stretched out his hand, motioning her to two chairs. "Please, come. Sit down. We have much to talk about. I mean you no harm."

"Who are you?" The words forced out of her mouth of their own volition. She was starting to freak out. Her hands shook as she smoothed them over the top of her head.

She had no choice. The option to run left the minute his men locked the door to the studio. Something poked from the back of her brain. His face seemed familiar somehow, but she couldn't quite place him.

They sat down across from each other in two oversized chairs. He leaned into her space with his forearms on his knees. Caging her in, he demanded her full attention. His eyes had lost their glassiness. He looked at her like a rare piece of artwork, tilting his head to the side.

"I have only ever seen you from a distance. You are even more beautiful close up." He raised his hand to touch her face but then let it drop.

Jesus, he was a stalker.

"I am sorry for the loss of your father." He looked at her intently, gauging her response.

Alarmed, she pushed herself back in the chair, trying to distance herself. "How do you know about my father?" The mention of her father made tears spring to her eyes.

"I have known your father for a lifetime. Although I lost him years ago." He failed to hide the hurt on his face as his eyebrows pinched together. His mouth turned down.

She was bewildered.

He began wringing his hands. "Your father and I were good friends for many years. Almost like brothers. His greatest pride was always his artwork. It proved to be his greatest downfall."

Her cell phone rang, interrupting the moment. She never took her eyes off him as he shook his head from side to side. His jaw muscle twitched. Seconds ticked by as the studio phone began to ring. He clasped his hands together, barking out orders to his men. One of them went to the studio phone and ripped the wire out of the wall. Her cell phone rang again. Her heart beat with more urgency. Someone was desperate to get a hold of her.

"Turn off your cell phone. I want no more

interruptions for us." The sharpness of his voice let her know she couldn't refuse him.

She plucked the cell phone from her purse. He watched her. Smart man because she planned to leave an open line for Dean. Once she unlocked the phone, he grabbed it from her and shut it off.

He cut her off from the outside world, making sure she had no way to gain control of the situation.

His eyes begged her to understand. "Please don't fear me. I am not here to hurt you. I would never hurt you." He held her trembling hands in his, quieting her like a child. "Shh, it's fine. All good." He smiled briefly, showing his flawless white teeth.

Her lower lip trembled. A sob broke out. Her breaking point loomed closer. In the voice of a little girl she said, "What do you want with me?"

"Did you ever notice how different you are from your sisters? Umm? Your hair is blonder and your eyes are lighter." He said the words 'little angel' in Russian again as he reached out to catch her falling tears with his thumb.

"My name is Alek." He waited for her response. When she didn't, sadness covered his face. "This will be a shock and hard to believe, but I am your real father. You are of Russian blood, my angel. I've always had my eyes on you even though I couldn't be near you."

She let go of his hands and sat back, stunned by his confession. Her heart pounded in her chest. "You're wrong. My mama is…was dedicated to my father." Her anger spiked at his audacity.

"Yes. She was. She had few choices." He sat back, rubbing his finger across his chin. "You want proof."

"Yes." She stood her ground. This had to be some kind of joke.

"For your birthday, I would always send you something that had to do with pigs, including the book *Charlotte's Web*. You were so pink when you were little. You reminded me of a piglet."

Her will to stay strong broke. She covered her mouth. He couldn't have known unless he had seen her. All her baby pictures of her looked pink. "No." She shook her head back and forth. She pounded her hand on the arm of the chair. "No!"

"I gave you everything from a pig blanket to all the glass pigs you own. Whenever I would travel, I would look for a pig to send you."

She always thought those pigs had come from her mama. How could she let her believe that?

"I didn't want you to find out this way. For that, I am sorry." Genuine sorrow etched his face as he leaned back in his chair.

"How?" The word fell from her lips.

"Ah, your mother is beautiful. Your father left her alone for many long nights, pursuing his passion. You must understand. I loved your mother with all of my heart, but we could never be." His face remained stoic, but his loss came through his eyes.

She didn't care about the love he had for her mama. "My papa said he tried to protect me and you would come for me. Why now? What do you want from me?" Her fingers curled around the arm of the chair.

He looked down and rubbed his hands together. "I wanted you to know who your real father is.

But that will wait. Right now, I need to get the photograph you have of me and your father." His eyes were unforgiving.

"How do you know about that photo?" She grew uncomfortable with how much he knew about her. It dawned on her where she had seen him. "You're him. You're the man in the photo with my father."

"Yes, I am the man in the picture with your father. You keep it separate from the other pictures. Why?" His eyes hardened.

She bristled at his request. "You've always fascinated me and now I know why. You've been looking for it. You broke into my apartment and studio."

"Yes." His eyes grew dark.

"Why do you need it?" The pieces were falling into place.

Anger grew instantly in his face. In a low voice, bearing the teeth of his Russian accent he said, "You are not to ask why. Tell me where the photo is."

Frightened by his sudden change, their attention was pulled to the banging sound on the door.

"Leigha, are you in there? Open up." Dean's desperate voice tore at her.

Alek grabbed her by the arm, hauling her to the kitchen, and kissed her cheek. "Do as I tell you. Get on the floor and stay there. I will see you again, my little angel."

He ran for the fire escape on the far side of the studio as his men covered him. The shots rang out in the small space, making her scream. Dean charged through the door, followed by Mac and

Sean. She stayed on the kitchen floor and watched as if she were in the middle of a crime show.

Dean fired back. The bullets cracked through the air. But none came near her. He moved in her direction and then jumped back as his right shoulder recoiled. His body crashed down. His head ricocheted off the floor. Mac and Sean surged forward to go after Alek and his men.

"Stay where you are," he yelled to her.

Like hell. There was no way she wouldn't go to him. She began to crawl to him and knelt beside him. "Oh God, oh God, oh God. You've been shot. This is all my fault."

His eyes looked dazed. "You don't listen, do you? Are you all right? I got scared when I couldn't reach you. Then your phone went straight to voicemail." He tried to sit up, holding his shoulder. She pushed him back down again. The blood seeped through his fingers and onto the floor.

Mac and Sean crawled back through the window from the fire escape. They stood over him, assessing the damage. "Well, at least we know exactly who owns the Range Rovers," Mac announced casually.

"Who the fuck cares about the goddamn Range Rovers? He's been hit." She hovered on the verge of hysteria.

Mac shrugged, putting his gun back in the holster. "It looks like a shoulder wound. He'll be fine. Let's get him to a hospital. In this traffic, it'll be faster to drive him there than calling an ambulance."

Dean's face grew pale. He winced as they lifted

him to carry him to the car.

She stood there, shaking from head to toe. Numbness coated her. She became overloaded with emotions.

"Leigha." Mac's voice popped her bubble. "Dean needs you. You need to come with us."

CHAPTER 29

Leigha followed them to one of the company's Suburbans standing curbside. Sean ripped the back door open and they threw Dean in the backseat.

"Jump in. We gotta roll." Sean looked through her. She was a bystander to the scene.

She sat flush up against the window, staring at him. He looked at her through pained eyes. She couldn't get enough air in her lungs. Nothing in life prepared her for any of this. He closed his eyes and laid his head back, still clutching his shoulder.

"Here, put this on the wound. Apply as much pressure as you can." Mac handed her a clean towel. "I don't know if it's a through and through or if the bullet's lodged in his shoulder. But we need to stop the bleeding." He snapped his fingers. "Leigha, are you with me? He's going to be fine."

Her hands shook as she grabbed the towel from Mac to use on his wound. He turned to face forward and made a phone call. She pushed the towel on the wound. She heard him gasp and released her pressure.

"You're doing fine, babe. Keep holding it there

no matter what I say or do," he said on a raspy voice. He looked at her through hooded eyes and a faint smile. "We have a lot to talk about. Did you really think you could run from me?" His eyes closed as he slipped into unconsciousness.

"Mac! He's unconscious. What do I do?" Frantic and twisted on the inside, she tried not to relinquish her control to a God who couldn't possibly exist. But she prayed anyway. "Please, please, please. Don't take him too."

Mac turned to her. "Slap him in the face. Try to keep him awake. Come on, Dean, we're almost there. I called ahead. They know we're coming."

He refocused on Sean's driving. They bobbed and weaved through downtown traffic. At each turn they got thrown around. She tried to hold to something. A stream of curse words left Sean's mouth as the horn blared.

"Slap him in the face," she repeated under her breath. She had never, for any reason, slapped anyone.

She grabbed his face and shook his head, which lolled around like a bobble head. Tears streamed down her face as she slapped him lightly.

"Don't you dare leave me. You promised. You said you would stay. Damn you."

She slapped him hard across the face.

He sat up, surprised by his surroundings. Confusion covered his face.

"We're almost to the hospital. You need to stay awake. I had to slap you. I'm sorry." Her hand covered her mouth.

He gave her half a smile. "Oh, come on, babe, you enjoyed it just a little. You've always wanted to slap my smart mouth, right?"

"Stop kidding around. Don't leave me."

He jerked back as if her words had hit him.

"I'm not going anywhere, babe. Not this time." His face went slack. His eyes turned dark. In an instant he left her. His mind seemed to travel somewhere else.

The Suburban stopped suddenly, throwing them forward at the Emergency Room entrance. Two paramedics waited for them with a stretcher. They pulled her out of the car and grabbed him, carefully laying him on the stretcher. He had lost all color in his face. She couldn't tell if he was breathing. They flew through the doors away from her. Air left her lungs at the thought of never seeing him again. She clawed at the pain in the middle of her chest.

Mac took her by the elbow and said softly, "Come on. We're going to wait inside. Do you want me to call your sisters?"

She nodded. A fog surrounded her to insulate her from life's daily dose of emotional overload and out of control moments. Her heavy legs followed Mac to the waiting room. Grim faces accosted her, sending waves of grief to swallow her whole. She found a seat far away from everyone else. Sean and Mac flanked her but kept their distance. The sounds of muffled weeps barely dented the shield she put in place. The thought of him dying consumed her mind, body, and soul. The excruciating pain made her nauseous. Maybe this was what it felt like to love and then lose someone.

A commotion on the other side of the room

caught everyone's attention. Two women came barreling through, pushing people out of the way. Raquelle led as the princess warrior coming to save her sister. Mara ran a close second but had trouble keeping up. They both stopped in front of her as if they hit her clear wall.

Mac got up, kissed Mara on the cheek, and walked away with Sean. "We'll find coffee."

After a long silence, Raquelle commented first, "This is bad. This is very bad."

Her river of tears hadn't stopped since they'd wheeled Dean away. She sat up straight, hands folded in her lap, crumbling on the inside. The pieces fell too fast for her to rebuild. Her sisters witnessed her undoing. The rock finally broke apart after years of weathering.

Mara sat down next to her and folded her in her arms, placing her head on her shoulder. "Shh, it's going to be okay. We will get through this together. Raquelle, why don't you call Mama."

She sat up. "No."

Mara and Raquelle stared at her.

"She has enough going on. We can tell her later."

They dropped the subject but gave each other questioning looks.

Raquelle sat on the other side of her, rubbing her back. She let out a shuddered breath of relief. Her pillars of strength came for her this time. The control shifted to them and she gave it willingly. She couldn't handle all of this by herself. She required their help whether she liked it or not. Like assembling a bike for a child on Christmas Eve, it would take more than one person to put her together.

She managed to calm herself enough to stop the onslaught of tears. Mara released her as Mac and Sean returned with coffee for everyone and tea for her. She took the paper cup from Mac to warm herself. Coldness had taken root in her from head to toe. The heat from the tea warmed her hands but didn't spread any farther. Ice encased her heart, unwilling to crack until she saw Dean again. Mac's eyes kept coming back to her, begging for answers.

"You want to know what happened," she said without looking at him.

"You need to tell me what happened so I can put some of the pieces together. I can help you." His voice had lost its hardness, worn down by exhaustion.

She carefully recounted the events of the morning. He asked questions and she answered them. She omitted the part about the man being her father. That morsel she would save for her mother. Anger and sadness collided. She thought about the father she never knew all these years because of her mother's secret. She went back on her promise to her sisters about keeping a secret. This one was too personal. It needed to start between her and her mama.

The day lagged on as minutes turned into hours. She began to pace. Something was wrong. He should be out by now. A shoulder wound should be easy. Why was it taking so long? Mac's face began to grow dark with signs of worry. He had gone through his fifth cup of coffee, working on his sixth. The air thickened with tension each time the double doors of doom opened. Everyone's heads snapped up, hoping for news about their loved one. Each time news came they dissolved into disappointment. But she was relieved as the bad news escaped them.

"Is Mac Creighton here for Dean Wagner?" a doctor with blue scrubs splattered in blood called out from the double doors.

Mac stood and turned to him. "Yes. We brought him in. How is he?"

The group flocked around him in anticipation.

"He's going to be fine now. There were complications with the entry of the bullet and where it hit his lung. The lung collapsed. We had more to repair than we'd anticipated. We have the bullet for analysis. You can see him in about an hour or so in recovery." Done with the job of delivering the news, he walked back through the double doors.

She turned to Mac. "What does he mean about complications? I need more information."

"We'll find out more from the doctor when we see Dean. Be patient. I know it's hard."

In the late afternoon, exhaustion crept up on her as she slid to the floor. Strong arms caught her, sitting her in the chair. Sean stroked her hand as someone handed her a cup of water. She had never been so lost.

CHAPTER 30

The beeps filled his ears while the antiseptic fumes assaulted his nose. Dean's mind tried to grab at clues to fill him in on his situation. This wasn't his first visit to the recovery room. The dryness in his mouth made his tongue feel swollen and his throat scratchy. His shoulder throbbed weighing down his body and making it weak. His lungs only allowed for shallow breaths. He opened his eyes to a beautiful blond nurse hovering over him, checking his vitals.

"How are you feeling, Mr. Wagner?" She used her gentle, soothing voice.

"Like I'm going to vomit."

"Okay, so let's get you some Zofran. I'll be right back." She scurried out the door.

She rushed back in with a small bottle and syringe. The liquid got pushed into his IV and his stomach began to settle. He used the button to tilt the bed and take in his surroundings.

"I never do well with anesthesia. Thank you." His words slurred.

"There are some people here to see you. I can send one in at a time. Who would you like to see first?"

"The stunning blonde. You'll know who she is." He winked at her.

She blushed and left the room.

The knock came before she peered around the edge of the door. Her hazel eyes rimmed in red encased in dark circles were the most wonderful sight he'd ever seen.

"Hey, babe. You had me worried." His stomach rolled and his head hurt.

She sat down next to him. Without saying a word, she lightly ran her fingers down his cheek. Tears pooled in her eyes. "I thought I would never lay eyes on you again. At least not alive. This pain was worse than losing my father. I thought it would kill me. You didn't leave me. You came back."

Her words wrapped around his heart to the breaking point. He would make things right from his past. This time he would stay. Years earlier Sophia asked him to stay and he wouldn't do it. This time would be different. The strong woman before him needed him for him, not just for protection.

He gripped her hand and he kissed her palm, holding it to his face. "I'll always come for you. Not because you need me, but because you want me. Babe, we need to talk about what happened. And there's something I need to tell you about my past." His heart raced in his chest, waiting for her reaction. Her eyes told him she couldn't quite process what he was saying.

They sat staring at each other when the door flew open. The nurse charged in holding a syringe. "Time for some pain meds to keep you comfortable." She proceeded to ease the liquid into his IV line, leaving as swiftly as she'd come in.

A mix of fear and anger crossed Leigha's face. Her breathing became rapid. "I need to take care of something. You need to get some sleep so your body can heal. The others are waiting for you." She squeezed his hand as she stood up to leave. The urgency in her voice made him frown, curious to know what was so important. "I'll be back later tonight. I promise." She leaned down and kissed his forehead.

"Don't hide anything from me. Tell me what's going…" He wanted to say more but his tongue became heavy, slipping into a medically induced slumber.

CHAPTER 31

Leigha pushed the hair off his brow, letting her hand slide down to cradle his jaw. Her hero took a bullet to protect her. Her Wilbur to his Fern. Unbeknownst to her, many people were looking out for her. Her head whirled with questions about her life, which appeared to be a complete lie.

She pulled the stiff sheet and cotton blanket up to his neck. The winds of change whirled around her. She would be coming back a changed woman. He would be none too happy to find out she kept this from him. But she had no choice. She closed the door and looked for her sisters.

"I need you two to come by Mama's later tonight." Numbness grabbed hold of her at the thought of what she had to do before they got there.

Her armor of control locked itself back in place for the battle awaiting her. It may not be necessary. She needed to listen to Mama with an open mind and heart. They stood silently, looking at each other and then back at her. Her hands opened and closed at her sides. She didn't need questions right now.

"Yeah, we can come by. What's going on, Lei?" Raquelle spoke for both of them.

"You'll find out when you come over. I need to speak with Mama first. Can I borrow your car?" She wore her mask of indifference. There would be no argument.

Raquelle threw her the keys. "Back of the parking lot. Be careful with my baby."

"See you soon." Why Raquelle drove an Aston Martin DB11 in the city, she would never understand. She turned and walked down the hall, gathering the courage she needed to face her mama's secret life.

She walked fast down to the parking lot without drawing attention. Her breath hit the unusually crisp air forming small clouds. They disappeared as soon as they formed like the events of the day. Her white knuckles gripped the steering wheel as she made her way to her truth. She needed to nail down her life. It had started with her father, but it would end with her mama. No one would be saving her from the conversation that would uncover who she really was.

The earlier phone call between her and Mama was filled with thorns. Her mama wasn't surprised by her request for answers to her questions.

She pushed open the unlocked front door and let herself in. The darkness of the house made her question her childhood memories as she weaved her way to her destination. She stepped into the den. Mama sat in Papa's chair in front of a blazing oversized fireplace.

"Come in and sit with me, *mi bambina*. I know

you need answers to many questions."

Her mama stared at the flames, lost in their dance. The warm light in the room shined on her. Sadness encompassed her. Life had thrown one too many punches. Leigha's heart hurt at the sight, but she needed to move forward.

She sat on the other side of her in the matching high-back chair. The table between them displayed a black box with a gold ice pick. An open bottle of Elit Stolichnaya vodka stood next to it. The amber-colored flames lit the side of her mama's face, casting the other side in darkness. She sipped from her crystal tumbler. The tumbler sparkled, catching the light of the fire through its many facets.

"I don't recall that I've ever seen you drink vodka." Her words broke the ice between them.

"The taste brings back too many memories. I dreaded when this day would come. I hoped it wouldn't come this soon." Mama's eyes were lost somewhere between happy memories and the fate of their moment.

They stared at the fire in silence. The wood crackled in the flames. A spark flew out as if to escape its inferno. If only it were that easy to escape. She didn't really want to have this conversation.

"My father came to visit me today. To say I was shocked would be an understatement. As he pointed out, I have his coloring, but you already knew that." Her voice sharp enough to cut as her accusation broke the surface.

Her mama cast her eyes at her with anger. "Don't judge me. You have no right to judge me until you've walked in my shoes. What Alek and I had was beautiful and happens once in a lifetime. I won't let you spoil my memory. You have led a privileged life because of all of it." The ice clinked in the glass as her hand shook. She brought the poison to her lips as a single tear slid down her cheek.

"Yes, privileged, caged, and unwanted." Bitterness laced her tone.

"Do you think you're the only one who lived that way?" She gave her a sideways glance.

Her body pulled back, shocked by the statement.

Mama continued, "I loved two men, your papa and Alek. Your papa is...was my best friend. But Alek was pure passion. If you are fortunate enough to find both in the same man, hold on to him with everything you've got." Her brief smile faded. Something broke in her eyes. "Around the time Marabella came into the world, your papa became world-famous for his signature piece 'A Soul Within Light From Darkness.' I was younger than you are now, left alone with a newborn with colic. You don't know what it's like to care for a baby all on your own day and night. It's exhausting. Alek came to visit. He could see I needed help with Marabella. Eventually, he left on business, but he kept coming back. With each visit, we got closer. I remember him being handsome, funny, and nurturing. We fell in love and couldn't get enough of each other."

Her hand lifted to take her last sip of courage. She closed her eyes and tipped her head back savoring the memories. She extended her glass, requiring a refill.

Her eyes focused on her tumbler as it filled. "When I found out I was pregnant, I knew Alek was the father. I told Antonio. He said nothing and left the same day. I had no idea where he went but when he came back, it wasn't going to be good. When he returned, he had changed, hardened. His lifelong friendship with Alek ended. I never saw Alek again."

Tears flowed freely down Mama's face. Each tear ripped away the facade she lived with for some many years. Her words came with relief and understanding. She carried the weight of the secret in her heart.

She took a breath to continue her story. "The day you were born, your papa came in and looked at you. You were a bubbling pink baby with blond wispy hair and light eyes, reminding him of Alek. But I also saw the light in his eyes. He would try and love you." She looked up with sorrow consuming her eyes. "He did the best he could. Your papa led the classic tortured artist's life. This only added to his pain." Her eyes begged her to understand a decision she barely understood herself.

Leigha turned away, staring at the dying flames that still warmed the room. She tried to absorb everything that floated between them.

Her mama continued with her explanation. "Alek never laid eyes on you. I pieced things together. This was the agreement between him and Antonio. I never asked and Papa never said anything. Alek called you 'little angel' in Russian. I would take pictures of you and send them to him. He said you reminded him of a little piglet all wrapped in your blanket. He would send you something having to do with pigs for every birthday including the book *Charlotte's Web*."

"I know. He told me. I wanted proof that he was my father. Only you and he would have that information." The web entangled her, constricting her. With each move, she fought to get out.

Mama's face grew serious. "He tried to be a good man, but he's also dark and troubled." She left the words hang without further explanation.

"You really loved him, didn't you?" Sorrow clutched her chest. She realized the torture she put her mama through by having her tell her story.

"Yes. More than you can imagine." A small glimmer caught in her mama's eye.

"Is that why you hovered over me all the time?"

"I was very protective of you." She looked down at her tumbler, swirling the leftover pieces of ice melted in alcohol. "Your papa never fully accepted you as a Luccenzo. You weren't of his blood. Italians are a little protective of that. Come to think of it, so are the Russians." Mama smiled.

Silence stretched out between them as Leigha continued to digest all the new information.

Her mama looked her in the eyes. "Leigha, you were never unwanted. Please believe me."

She nodded, unsure she accepted the statement. "I felt unwanted."

Mama nodded. "Did you tell your sisters?" Her words came out on a plea.

"It's not my story to tell. That's up to you. They're coming over later." She played with her fingers, lacing and unlacing them. "This seems to be a night of true confessions. I need to share one of my own. Do you remember Ben, the photographer?"

"Yes." Mama sat up straighter in her chair gripping the arms of the chair. Worry blanketed her features as she waited for her daughter's tale.

"He drugged and raped me. If Alek has been watching me all these years then I think he took care of him."

"Oh my God. What do you mean took care of him?" The words fell from her lips.

"I think he had him killed. Dean ran a trace on Ben. He dropped out of sight. His family filed a missing person report that remains open." Her heart filled with mixed emotions of vindication and sorrow.

Mama's shaky hand put her glass down. Tears streamed down her face for the one tragedy she couldn't protect her daughter from. She stood up to hold her baby. Even though Leigha towered over her, nothing could replace a mother's loving hug.

"I am so sorry." She reached up to stroke her hair and pushed the stray strands out of her face. "I tried to be there for you always. But your father, he—"

Raquelle and Mara walked into the den and stopped cold at the sight before them.

"What's going on?" Mara asked tentatively.

"And since when do you drink vodka?" Raquelle blurted out.

"Shush, you'll find out soon enough," Mama mildly scolded her firecracker.

"Mama has something to share with you." She put her arm around her mother and pulled her in close.

"Why do I get the feeling we're all going to need vodka?" Raquelle poured out a small glass of vodka for everyone. They sat down to listen to Mama's untold love story.

CHAPTER 32

Her sisters listened to their mama's story with rapt attention, glancing over at Leigha every now and then. She curled herself up in the high-back chair. The refreshed dancing flames captured her attention. Her nervous system had taken quite a hit in the last twenty-four hours. Her mind spun, trying to catch up and process her new reality. She had a greater understanding for her papa's struggle in his relationship with her. He did the best he could under the circumstances. But in the end maybe his best wasn't good enough. The high-test vodka coated her raw nerve endings, dulling some of the pain. The pull between anger and want warred inside her. She wanted to know her real father, but he scared her.

A mother's intuition never took a rest as Mama broke into her thoughts. "Don't try to pursue him. I got the feeling from your…papa…he is a very dangerous man." She laughed under her breath. "I don't even remember Alek's last name. I don't think I wanted to remember. Some mama I am." There went her shot at a Google search on him.

Mara's tears streaked down her face as her

nervous laugh broke the tension. "Look at all of us. We're a hot mess when it comes to men." She wiped them away with the back of her hand.

Mama stood up. "Italian group hug is in order, *mi bellas*." Like a soft blanket, their arms surrounded Leigha in comfort. Peace sank in her reveling in their comfort.

"I think you're a fantastic mother. Look at what you've been through. It couldn't have been easy to be married to Papa."

She understood her mother's loneliness. She came to the house angry but would leave with more understanding than she thought possible. Mama didn't end up with the man she was passionate about. She ended up enduring a life with her part-time best friend. Sometimes it was necessary to endure the situation rather than fight it.

"Alek wants a photo I took of him and Papa. Do you know why?"

"I have no idea. None of it makes any sense to me. I know your papa and Alek had an arrangement, but I don't know the details." Mama shrugged it off as another unsolved mystery.

"I have to go back to the hospital to be with Dean. He did get shot trying to protect me." Her face warmed at the mention of his name. The empty spot in her heart seemed to be reserved for him. But she couldn't be sure where it would lead. Her heart tumbled around in an ocean of feelings.

"I think someone is in love and doesn't want to admit it." Raquelle winked at her. Tipping her glass, she stuck out her tongue catching the last drops of vodka.

"I think it might be too soon for love but thanks for sharing. Got to go. Ta." She left to tell the rest of her story to the man she may be in love with.

She drove to the hospital, thinking about the events of the last week of her life. In the end, they would be a drop in the bucket. That one drop rippled through everything and everyone in her life. Mac would flip his shit when he found out she didn't tell him the whole story. Too bad. Suck it up, buttercup. Her life took priority. All her ducks needed to be in a row. She still held onto her spider's web of control helping her cope with life's fastballs.

She entered the darkened hospital room without a sound. Wires hung from her rescuer like tentacles. A cotton blanket lay on the recliner next to his bed. He knew she would keep her promise and come back.

"Hey, everything okay?" Groggy and unfocused, he reached for her and she caught his hand. "Come here. Lie next to me." He moved over as much as he could.

She squeezed in, lying across half of his body. She didn't want to admit it, but she needed him and only him. Being with him was like coming home. Safety and trust was never in question. She could let down.

Her dam finally burst. The first sob broke through, leading the way for the deluge of pain. Her entire body shook and trembled. The sobs came from somewhere deep in her soul. All the emotions of rejection, control, abuse, and torment came out in one fluid stream. She didn't recognize her cries of pain. Two men altered her life dramatically. She would never be the same. The mixture of the pain of not knowing her real father and her love for Dean looked like double exposure. The lines blurred together. The pain had nowhere to go but out.

—◆—

Dean's thin hospital gown became soaked with her tears. Her pain seeped into him with every sob and cry of pain. His mind went back to Sophia, imagining her tears of pain. His hand balled into a fist. Anger reared its head. This time he would make it right.

She let go of everything she held on to with her tight reins of control. He held her tightly, rocking her slowly and reassuring her that everything would be all right. She started to calm down with shuddering breaths. Her body gave way as she molded into his body.

"Are you ready to tell me the whole story?" he spoke into her hair.

She looked up at him with bright hazel eyes rimmed in red. "How did you know?"

"I'm a trained operative, remember? Most people don't lie very well. Everyone has a tell. Just remember that." He tapped her nose with his finger.

"What's mine?" She sniffled.

"I can't tell you. It's above your pay grade." He chuckled.

"I'll tell you all about it tomorrow. If you're a good boy," she said coyly.

He pulled her closer, nuzzling his nose in her

hair. "Once I spring out of here, I'm going to show you exactly how good I can be."

He looked up as the door opened. A nurse walked in unannounced. "Oh, honey, you can't be in bed with him. He needs his sleep. Hop into the recliner."

She kissed him as he wiped away her salty tears. She stiffly got up and fell into the recliner. The blanket covered her and she fell asleep within seconds. His angel's eyelids flutter closed. Curiosity bit at him to know the rest of her tale. It couldn't be any worse than his.

He laid his head back on the bed. The time had arrived for him to tell her his story of guilt. His secret had eaten at his soul long enough. He wavered between wanting to keep his secret forever and not ruining what he started with Leigha, to breaking through to the other side of peace and happiness. Lies ate at him from the inside, including the ones he omitted. They weighed on his chest like an anvil, knowing that one day they would catch up with him. He fell into a deep sleep, resting for the rough road ahead.

The warm morning sun washed the light blue walls, making them lime green. He gazed up at the holes in the ceiling tile, wondering if their number matched the holes in his heart. War and lost love could do irreparable damage to a man's ego that had already been shattered by a ruthless father. He turned toward the recliner, trying to breathe in the ray of shining light in his life. His woman fought through everything and came out on top. He admired her strength and fortitude.

She looked so small wrapped up in the blanket. He laughed as he thought of pigs in a blanket. He reached over, trailing his fingers across her cheek. Her eyes opened to mere slits.

"Good morning." Her voice sounded like she smoked one too many cigars.

"Morning, babe." He could wake up every morning like this and never look back.

"How do you feel?" Her hand peeked out from the blanket as she pulled it down.

"Like I've been run over by the mother of all trucks." After a full night's sleep, exhaustion still consumed his body.

A smirk covered her face minus any trace of blush on her cheeks. "You need to rest. You owe me as I recall."

He tried to roll over on his side but one of the tentacles stopped him. "And you owe me a story of what really happened in the studio." He watched as her head disappeared under the blanket. "Leigha, talk to me."

She threw the blanket off of her. "After a hardy breakfast. I'm starving. All those emotions can work up an appetite. Let me go scrounge something up for us." She picked up her bag, gave him a peck on the cheek, and left without looking back.

He wouldn't push her. She would come to him in her own time. Patience was on his side. The sooner she told him her story, the sooner he would need to tell her his story. He dreaded that moment more than anything.

She returned shortly with the works. Anything beat hospital food. They ate in silence, glancing at one another in fear. He needed to quell the worry in her eyes.

"I can take whatever you have to tell me."

"I know. But I'm having trouble with it myself. The man you saw in the studio with me is my real father, my biological father." Her brows furrowed.

He stared at her, keeping his face in check to mask his surprise. Total focus was key to getting her to reveal more of her story.

"Keep going," he said in a soft tone.

She curled herself up in the recliner, settling in for a long story. Her story included everything from the time of the shooting to the conversation with her mama. He listened intently without interruption.

He held out his hand. "Come here, babe."

She climbed on the bed with him and nestled in his arm.

"You constantly amaze me. You've been through so much. Yet here you are taking care of me. This is a lot to take in all at once. You're so brave." His voice cracked. Brave women seemed to be a thing for him.

He stroked her hair as they sat in silence, except for the beeping lifelines connected to him.

The door opened as Mac walked in looking like a raging bull.

CHAPTER 33

"*We need to* talk, all of us," Mac barked out to them.

Mara stood quietly behind him.

Dean wasn't going to take his overbearing bullshit. "Back off, mate. Leigha's been through a lot in the last forty-eight hours. She needs time to absorb it all."

His words were like bullets, Mac's body deflated as his shoulders rounded. "I'm sorry. This case is making me crazy, especially when the people I care about are involved and getting shot at." His eyes focused on Leigha. "Mara told me about your...father. Would you sit with a sketch artist for a profile on him? If he's who I think he is, this case just got a lot bigger than I originally thought."

"Who do you think he is?" Leigha asked in a small voice.

"Alek Romanowski, but we don't know for sure." His jaw muscles twitched.

Dean jumped in, "Your father is the head of the Russian mob?"

She shrugged.

"Fuck all."

Mac walked over to the side of the bed. "Looks like you're getting out of here in a couple of days. We'll talk more then." His eyes went back and forth between Leigha and him. A slow grin came across his face. "You may have caught another one of the Luccenzo goddesses. Good luck." He strolled over to Mara and held her face in his hands as he kissed her deeply, murmuring something in her ear that made her smile.

Mara came over to Leigha's side of the bed. "How are you both doing?"

"I think the better question is, how is Mac doing?" His voice strained with concern for his teammate.

"He hasn't been himself lately. I think he's keeping information about the case even from me." Mara's face wrinkled with worry.

"Suddenly, it's all hitting too close to home for him. He's taking it personally, which makes it harder." He looked at Leigha.

Her eyes softened at his words.

"I'm going to let you catch up and heal. Call me if you need anything." Mara leaned in to give Leigha a hug.

Everyone's heads snapped up as the door flew open and Raquelle walked in.

"Hey, bulletproof, how ya feelin'?" Raquelle approached him, hugging a huge paper bag to her.

Mara crossed her arms over her chest as if the comment had been aimed at her. "Raquelle?"

"What?" Raquelle shrugged her shoulders.

"I think it's funny," he said as the three sisters turned to stare at him. "You can call me BP for short."

Laughter bubbled up from inside him and he couldn't stop. He was torn between holding his stomach or his shoulder because they both hurt. But he couldn't stop laughing as they joined him.

Tears ran down their faces. The overinflated balloon of tension sprang a leak, relieving the pressure. He needed to laugh. He needed some relief to the heaviness of the series of moments called his life.

His laughter started to calm down. "I needed that laugh more than you know. Thank you, Raquelle. You can give me your one-liners anytime."

"Well, given the fact that hospital food sucks, I brought you lunch from the local deli that has slammin' sandwiches. I think it might help you heal quicker." She winked at him. She set the bag down and started handing out the sandwiches.

The air seemed lighter since they broke down in laughter. He noticed the three of them had gotten closer, complimenting each other and saying how they will always be there for each other.

The next couple of days went by without any major event happening as he continued to get stronger. His doctors agreed to send him home as long as he had twenty-four-hour care. Leigha volunteered without hesitation. Her eyes lit up at the suggestion.

She took him back to her apartment and set him up in the guest room. Her reasoning included not wanting to accidentally roll into him during the night and hurt him. He would go along with it for now. As soon as the lights were out, he would sneak into her bed. The need to be near her overrode everything else. But he couldn't truly be with her until she heard his story. Then everything might change. He would risk it all to be rid of the monkey on his back.

"You've been oddly quiet since we've been home. Is everything all right?" Her hazel eyes darkened.

"Yeah, babe, I'm fine. Just a little tired. I think I'm going to go to bed."

Pain flashed in her eyes. Whether she recognized his lie or felt rejected, he couldn't be sure. He needed some alone time to think things, though. He gave her a chaste kiss and wandered to the guest room.

He got settled into bed with eyes wide-open. His mind continued to turn in eighteen different directions. He had rehearsed the lines he would say to her over and over again. But it didn't ease the guilt gnawing at him from his gut.

He gave up. He got up out of bed and went in search of a good bottle of whiskey. To his delight, he found an unopened bottle of Rare Cask Macallan. He carried his drug of choice to the living room, set it on the cocktail table, and sat back on the couch. Macallan always took the edge off and helped him relax. He needed to get some sleep, but it wouldn't happen with the gears from the past still at work.

"I don't think that's going to go very well with the pain meds." She took the bottle from the table and put it away. As she stood on the other side of the table, the moon shined through a window, casting her in a blue haze. She put her hands on her hips, ready for a battle. "It's your turn to talk." He couldn't ignore the ache in her voice.

"Truth. I'm afraid you might change the way you see me. I don't want to lose you. I've lost too much already. I need to move forward, but I can't do that without sharing this piece of me with you first." He forced out the words.

"We all have our secrets. Maybe it's about time I kept another one of yours. Besides, you already have two of mine. Let's even the playing field." Her hands fell to her sides as she clasped them in front of her.

He clutched and unclutched his hands in silent prayer, trying to put his thoughts together. As he looked up, he saw her determined eyes focused on him. They held compassion that made him think it might be okay after all.

"When I was much younger than my thirty-one years, I fell in love with a beautiful girl, Sophia. We were inseparable. She would call me at all hours of the night, asking me to come pick her up. She said she missed me too much and couldn't stand to be without me. A young man's ego loves that shit. Men want to be needed." He stopped to catch his breath. His mind reeled back to those moments.

He ran his fingers through his hair, spiking it up. All the pain of that time cut his heart to pieces using a blade from the past. If he was ever going to move on, he needed to tell her the whole story. His confessional. No holding back.

Her eyes reflected his pain sensing impeding disaster.

"Sometimes I would find small bruises on her

thighs. But she always explained them away. She was a soccer player and things happened on the filed. I didn't put two and two together. When I turned eighteen, I signed up for the military for dear old Dad. It was expected of me. I'm the fourth generation Wagner to sign up for duty."

His hand dropped to his knees as his fingers dug in to the point of pain. He paused, looked up to the ceiling, and prayed for the strength to get through the story he'd never told anyone. He dropped back to being that confused young boy again who had one too many decisions to make about his life.

He continued, "She begged me not to go. I'd never seen her like that. She never played the drama queen, ever. She even suggested that we get married. That she could go with me. My dad wouldn't hear of it. I knew we were too young to make that decision and I left." He swallowed down his pain. "I never heard from her again. She never replied to any of my emails."

The welded steel box he created to seal in the guilt melted away. But not before it left a burn mark on his soul. He begged for her understanding. The buried tears from many years ago came to the surface, breaking sacred ground. He never cried. Only the weak cried. With each tear he let go of how strong he had to be for everyone around him; his sisters, mother, and teammates.

"When I returned a year later, my mother sat me down and handed me a letter. It was Sophia's handwriting. She wrote about the abuse she suffered at the hands of her stepfather. He sexually abused her for years. She couldn't take it anymore.

She deemed me her savior for all those years. She loved me more than she loved anyone in her life. Those nights she called me saved her from him. Fool that I was, I thought she just wanted me. What killed me the most was she never told me what was going on. If she'd told me, I would have taken her with me. I would have married her. I would have saved her because I loved her."

The wetness of a tear crept down his cheek. He didn't care if she saw it because the relief lifted the elephant off his chest. He let go of his selfish, boosted ego and lack of intuition.

"She wrote the letter right before she committed suicide," he whispered, waiting for her to look upon him with a different set of eyes. The secret that had been slowly killing him over the years was out. She held it in her hands.

She gasped. "I'm so sorry. I can't imagine what she went through. That's a heavy burden to carry for any man."

She moved to him. He got up off the couch, folding himself in her protective arms. He held her tightly to him, afraid that if he completely let go, he would never be able to piece himself back together.

———◆———

He revealed his deepest scar. It ripped her open. Leigha imagined what it must be like to have the one you love take themselves away from you because of the secrets and pain that ran too deep. Sophia couldn't survive without him. She needed him to rescue her.

He held her like a vice, binding them with his torment. She listened to his quiet sobs. His chest vibrated on hers, intensifying her own ache. They stood there locked together. His secret spiraled inside her. She wasn't sure whose secret held more power over them. Letting them go resulted in the same end—pain followed by peace.

He unwillingly let her go as she brushed the tears from his cheek. His bloodshot eyes were lost and unfocused. "Is this what you meant when you said you couldn't do this again?"

"Yes. I could have saved her life and her pain. Imagining what she went through kills me. God, I was such a fool," he said through gritted teeth. His eyes were those of an angry teenager.

"You were young. Why would you even guess she was being abused? She kept her secret well hidden. You weren't a fool. You didn't know." She continued to stroke his face, catching his tears with her fingertips.

He held her hand to his face. "Never again. No secrets, Leigha, ever. Are we clear?"

"We're very clear. Besides, you're the keeper of all of mine." She took his hand and led him to her bedroom.

No words were spoken. They stood in the darkness. She didn't need to see him. He bared his soul. The light within him broke free through his cracks. She untied his pajama bottoms and let them pool to the floor.

"Babe, you're going to have to be gentle with me."

She could feel his smirk even in the dark. "Oh, I plan on being very gentle with you. Now that I have your secret, I'm not letting go. It's safe with me." Her hands skimmed over his warm skin.

He kissed her as if he were sucking the life from her soul. Even with one hand, he easily stripped her down to her birthday suit, her favorite outfit. His free hand roamed, caressing and pinching every part of her body. They each held a piece of the other's soul through a series of events out of their control, designed by fate. Two damaged people finding each other in the wreckage. There were no barriers between them. They stripped themselves down to their essences, the keeper of each other's secrets.

He turned her around to face the bed and pushed her to lean on her hands. She understood his need to take over. He entered her inch by inch from behind. He stroked her back and cupped her breast. The tears welled up in her eyes. She wasn't sure where they came from. The intimacy of the moment threatened to consume her. She didn't need to see him. She needed to feel him. In a short time, he changed her, becoming the sun to her Venus.

He stopped moving and pushed her hair to one side. "Making love has never felt like this with anyone. I would move heaven and hell to be with you." His voice was the blade of a knife.

She peeked over her shoulder at him. The full moon had positioned itself to shine on him. She could see determination in his eyes. He kissed her with a tenderness that clutched her chest and wouldn't let go. He wiped her tears away without asking what they were about.

Her emotions ran too deep. She knew it wouldn't

take much for her to detonate. He went slowly as if he wanted to remember every movement. He stroked her clit just the right way. His low moan indicated he was close as she connected with him. They came together, falling on the bed in a blissful heap. He held her around her arms, tucking her into him.

"You're amazing," he mumbled into her hair.

"Funny, BP, I was thinking the same thing about you."

They laughed together.

"Let's give our weary souls a rest."

Tomorrow could wait along with any other secrets like her father's next move.

CHAPTER 34

Leigha had a better understanding of what made him tick. His face softened, resembling a young man who had come to terms with his past. He slept soundly as if he had been overexposed, in need of regeneration. Their pieces began to meld together. She slung her arm over her eyes. Rest. Peace.

The trill of her cell phone made her jump. She didn't recognize the number but with the way things had been going lately, she couldn't ignore it.

"Hello?" she spoke softly not to wake the slumbering bear next to her.

"Little angel." His voice held tenderness, but the hair on her arms stood on end. She slid out from under the covers and tiptoed across the room to the kitchen.

"How did you get my number?" She tried to hide the irritation in her voice.

"I will always be able to find you. But we don't have time for that now. I need the picture of Antonio and me. Leigha, you must not tell anyone about this." His sharp voice made it clear he was done with his fatherly duty.

She sensed she shouldn't be pushing him, but his request seemed odd to her. "Why do you need it?"

"I'm in a business where no one can know what I look like, even in an old picture. You possess the only one out there for my enemies to get." The confidence in his voice made him sound convincing. "I need to get the photo from you as soon as possible…"

"You'll excuse me if I don't jump to your commands, but my…boyfriend got shot by one of your men. I'm not leaving him until he recovers." Who did he think he was? She only found out recently that he was actually her father.

"And one of my men got killed, so I would say we are more than even. I'll see you tomorrow. Union Square, three o'clock. You must come alone, otherwise we both could die or one of your half-sisters if you don't show." He clicked off before she could reply. The silence on the other end reeked of fear he left in his wake.

She stared at the phone in disbelief, rubbing her thumb over the keys. He made his threat clear.

"Who was that?" Dean's stern voice caught her off guard. She spun around in his direction.

He leaned against the doorframe, shirtless, with his sweatpants hanging low on his hips. Even with his shoulder all wrapped up, he still looked delicious. His eyes narrowed, waiting for her response. After he shared his past with her last night, he still anticipated she might lie to him.

She stood up to her full height and looked him in the eye. "Alek. He's demanding the photograph of him and my…papa."

His eyes focused on her and held doubt. "Did he say why he needs it so badly?"

"Apparently, it's one of the only photos out there of him. He's trying to keep it from his enemies. Something feels off, though." She laid her phone on the counter.

"Let's take a look at this photograph." His tone softened.

"It's taped up inside my nightstand." She brushed by him, hit by a spark from the night before.

He grabbed her by the waist and pulled her in tight. "Thank you," he whispered in her hair.

"For what?" She curled her head in his neck.

"For everything. Last night, this morning. I heard some of your conversation with him. He didn't want you to tell anyone, did he?"

"Yes, but no secrets, remember? Besides, my Spidey senses are tingling." Anxiety spun in her stomach.

She pushed away from him and plucked the bagged photo from the top of the drawer.

He carefully eased the photo from the bag. She held her breath. She knew why feelings were attached to that photo.

He looked at the photo intently, running his thumb along the top as his fingers brushed the back. The photo was on thick paper with worn edges. His brows furrowed questioning what his digits were telling him. He turned the photo over. All she saw was a white back.

———◆———

"Shit." Dean moved around the bed, searching for his phone. He grabbed it from his jeans pocket, pressed two numbers, and walked quickly to the living room.

"I need you to come over, Seven. Bring Iceman. Rear entrance."

"Roger that."

Every agent at MBK had been given a code name. When the code names were put in play the situation changed dramatically, boosting it to a high level of importance. Iceman was the name for Peter Bryan, one of the other MBK partners, their insanely intelligent IT guy.

He fell onto the couch, staring at the back of the photo. He rubbed his thumb over it again and again. Recognition hit him but had no clue to what it was about.

She stood in the archway to the living room with her arms crossed over her chest.

"What's going on?" Her voice filled with fear and suspicion.

"We'll find out when Mac gets here with Peter." He looked up at her. Her eyes widened as she read the fear in his. "This is way bigger than we thought. You have something he desperately needs."

Her hand ran along the top of her head. "I'll go make us some tea and coffee. It looks like it's going to be a long day." She turned away without looking at him. Her body hung like a sweater that had been worn one too many times.

The knock at the door came fifteen minutes later. Mac entered with Peter wheeling in behind him. He operated his chair like an extension of his body. His green eyes shone from under his auburn hair. He looked over at Leigha holding a tray of drinks.

"She's taken, cowboy." Peter's charm went a long way with the ladies. He needed to shut him down.

He raised his hand in surrender, giving her a sheepish grin. "Okay, okay."

Mac rolled his eyes. "Can we cut to the chase? What's suddenly so important?"

He handed the photo to Peter. "Take a look at the backside. See anything unusual?"

"It's a security chip. What the hell is a security chip doing on the back of an old photo? Do you know what's on it?" Peter began looking at it from every angle.

"No, Einstein. That's your job. We have until three o'clock tomorrow to figure this out. Alek wants his photo back. He's threatened Leigha's sisters."

He looked up in time to witness Mac's face go dark with rage. It was just the reaction he was looking for from him.

Mac's voice turned icy. "Is that so? Even with Leigha's description of Alek, we still can't verify that it's Romanowski. My guess is that he went dark years ago. We'll change out the chip and hope he doesn't notice. If he's been keeping tabs on her all these years, we can't send someone in her place. He'll know immediately. Leigha, I want you to make the drop. Do you think you can do it? You'll have plenty of backup."

He bolted up off the couch, getting within inches of Mac's face. "No. Fucking. Way. Mate.

She's not going anywhere near this guy or doing the drop."

Mac took a step closer sharing his air. "She has no choice. It's the only way we can bring this guy out in the open. I'm not putting anyone else in jeopardy with this. We'll cover her with other operatives from the firm."

He felt her hand on his forearm pulling him away.

"I can do this. I actually want to see him again. I don't really know why. But he's my blood. He pushed me onto the floor of the kitchen to keep me from getting hurt at the studio. I don't think he'll hurt me." Her eyes filled with determination laced with sorrow.

"Babe, I can't cover you. I'm not healed. He knows me. It would put everyone in danger." He gently held her upper arm.

"It's time for you to trust the ones around you. I've seen Mac in action. I trust him with my life. It'll be fine." She held herself with confidence like a woman on the verge of a new discovery.

"I'm going to go back and work on this right away. I want to pull the information off of this, duplicate it, and replace it." Peter put the photo in his pocket then turned to head out the door.

Mac released a breath. He held the bridge of his nose with his finger and thumb. "We need a break in here somewhere. Peter's a friggin' genius when it comes to this stuff. I have total faith in him. He'll be ready by tomorrow. We need to be on our game. In the meantime, stay in lockdown today." His eyes showed the weariness of the case.

He followed Mac to the door, closed it behind

him, and turned the lock. He reached for his salvation and folded her in his arms.

"I don't want you anywhere near this. But I don't have a say, do I?" He choked on his words. If things went south, no needle and thread could sew him back together.

CHAPTER 35

The morning light filtered through the blinds like any other day. Leigha wished today were any other day. Her nerves were sparks at the end of a wick. She rolled over, expecting to be greeted by his handsome face. Instead, he sat on the side of the bed with his head hung low. Hearing her move, he looked over his shoulder. His hair spiked out everywhere, the tell tale signs of a restless night's sleep. The dark rings around his eyes accentuated the profound sadness in his light blue eyes. It speared her to think she might be the cause.

"I need you to come back to me. I can't do this again. I can't lose you. There will be nothing left of me. I will become the abyss." He turned his body toward her and leaned on his hand. "Leigha, don't come within striking distance of him. Don't let him come close enough to grab you. I'm not sure he wants just the picture. I think he wants you. With your father out of the way, he can be in your life." His words hung on a plea.

She sucked in a breath. The thought never occurred to her she might be setting herself up for a kidnapping. "I hate to admit that I never thought he wanted to kidnap me."

A small smile graced his lips. "That's why you have me now. Come here."

He reached out to her. She got up to sit next to him on the bed. His arms enveloped her in a cocoon of protection. His eyes shut tightly as if praying to whatever god would listen.

"Open your eyes. I'm coming back to you. I wouldn't be surprised if Mac doesn't have the entire NYPD covering me. You're the only place I want to be. You found something in me I didn't even know existed. You proved I can depend on you. Now, you need to depend on me to see this through."

His eyes softened as she stroked his jaw and peppered it with kisses.

"I've got some things to do at the studio. I think you should come with me. Get your mind off all of this for a while."

Without a word, he got up and took her hand, leading them to the bathroom. Since his injury, he required a lot more of her help. The shower had turned into their alone time where they could steal themselves away from the rest of the world. She treasured being in a bubble with him. She took in every sound he made as his body hum with satisfaction.

The rest of the day remained quiet between them. Every so often he would kiss the top of her head and rub her back. She wasn't sure if the gesture was for her reassurance or his. Even with the physical contact, she could feel him distance himself in anticipation of her disappearance. She had every intention of coming back to him come hell or high water.

The downstairs buzzer sounded, shaking her out of her work mode. He got up to answer the door. A baritone voice overpowered his voice as an argument ensued. She left her proof table and made her way to the front of the studio.

"Mac says you're to stay here." A tall black man built like a MMA fighter towered over him. She didn't think many people won any arguments with him.

Dean gritted his teeth. "And I say I'm not letting her out of my sight."

She got between them and extended her hand. "Hi, I'm Leigha. Nice to meet you."

He took her hand in his, holding it like porcelain. "I'm Beck McKenzie, the M in MBK. I wish we were meeting under different circumstances. I'm your bodyguard for the day." His English accent gently rolled off his tongue. It put her at ease. The deep scars on his face didn't detract from his chiseled cheeks and thousand-watt smile. She was in good hands.

He turned back to deal with Dean. "Mate, if her contact sees you, all bets are off. Peter worked all day and night to perfect this chip. This op has to run smoothly. Don't make me find you a babysitter." He crossed his arms over his broad chest, resting his case.

"Fine. But I'm not happy about it. Take care of her with your life."

"With my life, mate. No worries. Besides, I owe you." Beck reached out and hugged Dean into his chest. She stepped back at the unexpected move.

"Let's roll, love."

"Hey, watch it. That's my love and only mine. I don't share."

"That's not what I heard." Beck turned, giving him his shoulder, ready for the punch. His hearty laugh filled the small space. Dean punched him in the arm. He didn't even flitch. "We'll meet you back at her place, soon." He winked. He took her by the arm and guided her downstairs to the waiting car.

She wanted to dig her heels in like a kid who didn't want to go to the big event. Her mind whirled with hundreds of scenarios, none of which ended well. Stumbling in the lobby, Beck stopped her.

"You're going to be fine. Trust." He winked.

A black Suburban waited at the curb with blackout windows. Beck opened the door. She slid across the seat and he moved in after her. Mac sat on the far side, concern etched on his face, his work mask firmly in place.

"We're going to drop you off at the subway station a couple blocks from Union Square. You're to take it to 14th street, the Union Square stop." He stopped to rub his thumb across the scar at his eyebrow.

"I know the rest." She focused on her gripped hands.

The text she received earlier in the day gave directions. He would meet her at the bench to the left of the Abraham Lincoln statue under the tree. He wanted a public area with some privacy.

Her hands laced and unlaced. She took deep breaths. Mac's warm hand covered both of hers.

"You are well covered. I'll guard you as if you were my sister. I won't let anything happen to you." Sadness covered his eyes at the mention of his sister, Kendall.

"Dean said I should keep my distance in case he tries to grab me." She looked down at her running shoes.

"After what we found on the chip, I'm sure he's desperate to have it back. What's on there has nothing to do with his picture. We ID'd him." He had a hard look in his eyes. "He's a very dangerous man, Leigha. I need you to give him the photo and walk away. Do you understand?" His hooded eyes grew darker, trying to hide his fears. He handed her the photo in its plastic bag.

She nodded. Her head felt light. She couldn't inhale enough oxygen. The situation had intensified in a couple of sentences. "I don't know if I can do this." A hard lump formed in her throat.

"You can do this. I watched how strong you were in Mexico. The fact that you are his daughter means something to him. He won't hurt you. He doesn't need the extra baggage of kidnapping you. Sorry." He cringed at his choice of words.

The SUV stopped abruptly and Beck opened the door. The light from the street cut through her veil of protective darkness. The reality of the situation hit her full force.

She stepped out into the street with voices, honking horns, and laughter swirling around her. Her hand rose to cover her eyes, shielding her from the onslaught. The slam of the car door startled her as the strong wind of fate pushed her from behind. She started to move down the subway stairs that threatened to make her disappear. Fear gripped her like a vice, promising to cut off her lifeline. Dean swam in her mind as tears formed in her eyes. How could she find him, almost lose him, and put her life in danger all in one fell swoop? No. Fuck that. She would be the person winning at this game. Alek would get what he wanted. Then she never wanted to be near him again.

The subway car stopped in front of her. With every step, she found more resolve in her mission. She would use her new control to her advantage. She dug deep to grab hold of it and lock it down tight. Genetically speaking, she was made of some pretty tough stuff.

A businessman sat across from her, giving her a menacing smile. Her model good looks caught his attention. As he stared at her eyes, their frost gave way and his smile faded.

Leaning her arms on her knees, she looked him straight in the eye and said, "Fuck off." Never taking her eyes off of him, she leaned back as if it were just another day on the subway. The string pulled tight inside her, ready for almost anything at this point. She was tired of the manipulations in her life.

The announcement for the 14th street stop blared through the speaker. She got up to take her leave. She walked up the stairs and across the park. Determination guided her to the tree covered path and her father. Up ahead stood a statue of the man who represented truth. A laugh bubbled to the surface at the irony.

A blunt object pushed into her back.

"Don't turn around." He laughed. "God, that's

so cliché. Walk to the bench up ahead and sit down. My men are covering every inch of this place."

Her resolve began to fade. Her nerves shook under the surface. She sat down in the middle of the bench. He sat close enough to her that his leg touched hers. She slid away from him, creating some distance between them.

Her eyes met his hazel ones she recognized as her own. He donned a hat and looked older since she had last seen him. His face revealed a man who lived many lives. Paid many dues. Trapped in his web.

The words little angel traveled on the cold breeze. "I would never hurt you. I've spent a lifetime protecting you, wishing I could know you. But we weren't meant to be. You are my only daughter. I'm so proud of you. You are strong, intelligent, and in control. Your choice in lovers isn't so great, men or women." He stopped and cocked his head to the side, letting his words sink in. But she didn't waver.

Her eyes never left his face. She wanted answers. "Did you do something to Ben?" She held her breath afraid of his reply.

"He gave me no choice. He hurt you. I blame myself for not being able to stop him." He raised his chin in defiance.

Her jaw tightened.

The sound that filled the space between them was two swallows arguing on a branch above them. She thought of the birds on Dean's shoulders. Her father had tried to let her know he was always there for her.

He sighed, "Your mother is my biggest regret. She's my one true love, always." He looked at the horizon as if remembering another life. "We had magic and passion. The kind of magic you find once in a lifetime." His head snapped in her direction. "Don't blame her. You don't know what she went through with your…father."

"I don't judge her. My…papa wasn't an easy man to live with." The questions bombarded her but remained out of reach.

"You can blame me for that. My life is complicated. So was Antonio's." Darkness fell over his eyes, hiding his secrets. He changed tact. "Do you have the photo?"

"Yes." Her hands shook in her pockets as they searched for the plastic bag.

She pulled out the bag and handed it to him. He put it in his pocket without a glance.

He reached out to cradle her face in his warm palm. "I don't know when I will see you again. You will do well with Dean. He has demons but nothing he can't handle."

Tears sprung to her eyes. He almost broke her in pieces. She found him only to lose him again, conflicted between him as her father and the criminal. She stood up. "I have to go."

"Yes, I know. If you stay much longer, the troops will come to save you. Be well, my little angel." He smiled, but it didn't reach his eyes. She sensed that regret was the only thing that lived in his soul.

She stared at him in awe. He had answers to questions she hadn't even asked. She walked backward at first, then turned and jogged out of the park. She couldn't stay to watch Mac and his gang arrest the father she would never know. Her heart sobbed for all the things she would never have with him. Tears streamed down her face as her legs burned, trying to keep up with her spiraling emotions. Not sure where to go, she needed to keep running.

CHAPTER 36

Leigha's feet hit the pavement hard, sprinting up Park Avenue South to East 20th street. She would find peace in her favorite place in the city. Gramercy Park was a small but quaint spot encircled by modern and turn of the century architecture. One could hide in its lush foliage. The sun streaked through the leaves to warm her face. She collapsed on a bright green bench trying to catch her breath. No one would find her here. This was the secret hideaway she kept from everyone, even her sisters.

She tried to relax with the cool breeze but couldn't outrun her scattered emotions. There weren't many people in the park, which was a blessing. Her eyes took in various things from plants to the gravel pathway but stopped on the statue. Edwin Booth stood before her, an American actor, as he played Hamlet.

She felt the bench move next to her. Without looking over she said, "How did you find me? This is my secret place. No one knows about it." Her eyes met his brilliant blue eyes filled with sadness.

"I hate to admit it, but I tracked your phone. It doesn't make me a stalker. Actually, maybe it does. But I couldn't let you go without knowing you were okay. You see, you've placed a tracker on me as well. You fill the part of my soul I thought died years ago. You breathe life into me and challenge me. God, do you challenge me."

His beautiful smile lit up her heart looked blurry through her tears. She let out a deep sigh. Someone found her, all of her, and wanted what they saw.

"Today has been filled with irony." She looked up at the statue of Edwin. "His acting ability had been overshadowed by his famous brother John Wilkes Booth's assassination of Abraham Lincoln." She paused. "Kind of like being overshadowed by my father all these years and not even knowing it."

She had run from honest Abe to the brother of his killer. Honesty had been killed that day. In the short amount of time she knew her father, his truth came in many colors to suit his situation. He was involved in things she couldn't even comprehend. She didn't want to be part of his world. She wanted to be in his presences for a little bit longer. Questions without answers floated in her mind and quickly disappeared. Her head hung at another one of life's disappointments.

He lifted her face so the sunlight kissed her skin. His thumb wiped away her tears. "Let him go. He may have overshadowed you, but he'll only ever be a ghost. He never made himself visible to you. He won't now either." His lips brushed gently against hers as a reminder of her fragility. "I love you. That's a promise I will keep forever along with your secret park." He smiled at knowing another one of her secrets.

She crumbled in front of him. He picked up her pieces. He cradled her in his good arm. They sat listening to the songbirds in the middle of the chaos of the City. With her ear pressed to his chest, she listened to him breathe. She tried to match her breath to the rise and fall of his chest. She could stay there forever, taking in every nuance of the park from the trees to the wilted roses at the end of their cycle.

The ring of his cell phone broke the beauty of the moment. "Yes. Of course I'm with her." He raised his voice. "Because I'm not letting her out of my sight, that's why. We're on our way." He closed the phone as his eyes became hooded with worry. "We need to go back to Mara's apartment. Mac's called a meeting. He sounded somber and more than a little pissed." He shrugged.

She knew he wasn't supposed to be with her. She nodded her head. Reluctantly, she agreed to have her day of disappointments continue. They stood and walked hand in hand out of the park to hail a cab. They slid in the backseat. She buried her head in his good shoulder, praying he would skip the meeting and drive them to the beach again. He was nothing if not loyal. They would be going directly to Mara's apartment.

Cars jammed the street, so they walked a block to the high-rise. The silence between them hung in the air, waiting to be pierced.

"You're very quiet. You want to talk about it?" He said it without pressure.

"I'm drained. I can't imagine what Mac has to tell us. He got what he wanted—Alek."

"Well, not exactly."

She stopped a couple feet from her sister's front door. "What do you mean? Did Alek escape?"

"Yes and no. Let's say we have him where we want him. I'll let Mac explain."

Silence encased her again as she tried to imagine what mac had up his sleeve. Voices leaked through the door to Mara's apartment. She recognized Raquelle's loud voice chewing out Mac's ass for losing her sister. It made her smile. She knocked two times before the door swung open with Raquelle on the other side.

"Where the hell were you? We've been going crazy here."

Before she could answer, Raquelle grabbed her in a bear hug. She watched as Mara strode across the room toward them. She peeled Raquelle's arms off of her to give her a hug.

"Well, I'm here now." She turned away from Mara, ready to confront Mac. "Do you have Alek or not?" Her fingers gripped her hipbones. After a day of spiked emotions, she would stand her ground.

"Yes, but not physically. Peter, boy wonder, placed an untraceable tracker in the chip. We're following Alek. I need him to show me the bigger picture of what he's involved in. There are implications to the Russian government as well as other things. We haven't sifted through it all yet. It's highly encrypted. I can't thank you enough for what you did. You're incredibly brave."

She nodded, trying to process everything that

had happened. Dean's hand caught her elbow and he guided her to the couch.

"Why don't you sit down while I make you some tea in your favorite piglet tea cup?" He bent down, kissed her forehead, and made his way to the kitchen.

"I think you all had better sit down. I have some news you need to know." Mac's jaw ticked. He closed it tight as if he were trying to hold it together.

She looked at her sisters for answers. Puzzled looks covered their faces. They were in the dark with her. Sitting on either side of her on the couch, they each grabbed one of her hands. Together they stood and together they would fall.

Dean came back in the room and sat in the chair opposite her to make sure he was in her line of vision.

Mac stood in front of them. "First off, Alek Romanowski is the head of the most powerful Russian mob family. When I say family, I mean they are all involved in one way or another. There are five generations of Romanowskis. You might say it runs in their blood. Sorry, Leigha." Confusion crossed his face. "I hate that my business life has mixed with my personal life on many different levels. It sucks."

"It's okay. Please continue." She wanted to hear every gory detail about Alek.

"Sydney was brought up by her Armenian uncle who has strong ties to Alek's family. They trained her to be a double agent starting at ten years old." He pinched the bridge of his nose and took a deep breath.

"At least she never took you out. She seemed almost protective of you. She had some redeeming qualities." She needed to come to her defense. She couldn't believe Sydney was steeped only in evil.

"Yeah, don't think that hasn't crossed my mind on more than one occasion. She had every opportunity. I've gone over our missions a million times in my mind. If nothing else we have a better understanding of what she signed up for without knowing. I don't think she had a choice. Unfortunately, she got caught in the crossfire and became expendable." He sat down in the other chair opposite the couch. His body folded in on itself.

He rubbed the scar above his eye with his thumb then folded his hands in prayer over his nose and mouth. Leigha recognized his tells. A bombshell was about to go off.

"For God's sake, out with it already. I can't take it." She squeezed her sisters' hands.

"We got the tox results on your father. He was poisoned. The chemical had to be administered over time to make it look like the flu. That means someone close to him gave it to him without his knowledge." He looked each of them in the eyes. "I'm telling you this without your mother here because she's a prime suspect."

The sisters simultaneously let out a gasp.

Raquelle spoke first. "Are you fucking kidding me right now? My mother? Salt of the Earth? Rescues ants from being stepped on? This is nuts!"

"Look, I don't believe it either. But the police have to go in this direction first and rule out all possibilities. If I ran the investigation, I would look at your mother too."

"It's not Mama. What would her motive be at this point? She endured my father for over thirty years. He was ready to retire, which she was happy about." Mara made a good point.

"I don't know where they're going to go with all this. But I wanted you to know so you could be there for her. It's going to be a tough go." Mac rubbed his hands together. "There are still some missing pieces having to do with Brock and CZR Investments. We're hoping Alek can lead us to more answers. This isn't over."

She looked at her sisters. Wariness covered their faces. They would walk on a broken road with no smooth surfaces ahead. But they would stand together as they added to their family unit, waiting for the next strike.

———◆———

*I*f you missed Marabella and Mac's story, here's an excerpt...

TRUTHS

*M*ac *staggered down* to the pool of his all-inclusive resort and flopped into the closest lounger. Beyond exhausted and head pounding, he laid back on the lounger. His first night in Cancun had him 'get his drink on' with a couple of ladies in attempt to forget about the enticing Marabella.

The five-star resort boasted spectacular surroundings but he couldn't get into it. He would have to take it all in later when his mind wasn't so muddled. This trip to Mexico had been his only vacation in five long years. His never-ending marathon had him burned out and running hard. The scattered pieces of life's disappointments needed to be put back together. Even on vacation, the agency managed to give him one more assignment.

Pushing himself up into a sitting position at the edge of the lounger, he hung his head in his hands. A tiny prickle on the back of his neck caught his attention. He scanned the area across the pool.

Squinting to sharpen his focus, he wanted to make sure he was seeing things correctly. He scrubbed his face with his hands. Yep, that was her. Marabella. The beauty he couldn't forget about no matter how hard he tried. His hands balled into fists. She was his first thought that morning even after a night of tits and tequila. How could he ever forget how she affected him? Releasing his hands, he folded them in prayer over his nose and mouth. He breathed out heavily, trying to figure out his next move. The pull to her was automatic and without rationale.

Two women stood next to her. He assumed they were her sisters. They had pushed their way toward her on the plane as he made his escape. But neither one of them moved him the way Marbella did. The mystery woman piqued his curiosity. She rolled over him like a warm ocean wave that lulled you to a peaceful place down to your soul. Stirring his emotions, she took him off-balance. The gods of torture had placed her right in front of him. He preferred friends with benefits for a reason. No one got hurt. But he couldn't turn away from her. This was either going to be one hell of a train wreck or the most beautiful sunrise ever.

He studied her from across the pool. Her sisters walked away, leaving her to play with something in her lap. She wore a black one-piece bathing suit with a short pink sarong exposing her well-toned legs and generous cleavage. She focused on her hands but the sadness never left her face. It traveled across the pool in waves, punching him in the chest. An empty umbrella drink sat next to her. He wanted to disprove the hold she had on him. As he grabbed the pink drink from the outdoor bar, his hand shook slightly. Since when did he get nervous about getting a woman a drink? She was unfamiliar territory.

Wandering over, he glanced at the pool, imagining what it would be like to get her wet. He set the fruity drink down next to her and waited for her response.

She glanced over as recognition hit. Her eyes followed his big forearm with a smattering of dark hair upward to be confronted by his huge shoulders under a black t-shirt, messy brown hair. Goosebumps formed on her skin, as her breathing picked up. He hadn't even touched her.

"Is that drink for me, Mac?" Her soft tone held reserve.

"Aye, I'm not much of an umbrella drink kind of chap. I thought I would keep your appetite wet." He wanted to push her little, trying to gauge her reaction to his double entendre. Years with the company taught him that you needed to be able to read people well or suffer the consequences— which, in this case, may end with his shattered heart. His body tensed, aware of the tug between fight or flight. He wanted to walk away but staying seemed to be winning this war.

She peeked up at him from under her hat, her eyes soft and sincere. "I took you for more of a whiskey guy. Like the whole bottle, from the looks of it." She gave him half a smile. "I want to thank you for putting up with me on the flight. You're a real gentleman. There aren't many of those left in the world." Picking up her drink, she stirred it with the umbrella.

God, if she only knew, she would probably run for the hills. The dark side of him wanted to take her to edge to find out if he could bring out her wild side. He wanted to possess her until she screamed out his name, begging for release. Reel it in, mate.

"You don't need to thank me. It was my pleasure. By the way, are you trying to tell me I look like shit after a night of drinking?" He chuckled. "I guess it's a small world. How long are you here for?" His fingers dug into his hips. Those eyes with that body had him forgetting about any other woman on the planet. Dangerous territory. The dance between staying or fleeing continued.

"My sisters and I are here for ten days. I needed this getaway to rethink and recharge." Sadness pulled at her face.

"Do you mind if I sit down?" She nodded. He moved around her, pulling the lounger over so he was right next to her.

She gazed down at her piece of clay that started to take shape. He regarded the blob, wondering why she would bring clay to a pool. Then he remembered Eros, her safety net.

"I hope Eros had a safe landing. Do you take clay wherever you go?" he said with a serious tone.

Her chin came up. "For your information, I'm a sculptor and yes, I take clay wherever I go. It helps me think and unwind. My hands and head work together. They always have." Her gaze returned to the clay in her lap.

"Do you make anything else?" He leaned in to get a closer look.

Her head popped up and her smile made an appearance. "I've created other pieces like small pigs, lamb and fish. My collection grew over the years." Her fingers feathered over the red clay. "I donated one of my bigger free-spirit pieces to the hospital. Then they asked me to make something for the children's wing. I thought it would be a great opportunity to hand them out to the sick kids. Their smiles lit up their faces. They loved to touch the little sculptures." Her smile reached her eyes making them sparkle.

"I volunteer once a month to help the kids make their own creatures. I hope having their own muse would help them get through their illness. Making their own little creature is unique and colorful experience for them." Her smile slipped. "The two things that seemed to be missing in my life."

The knife struck his heart at the mention of sick kids. "So you're an artist?" His fascination continued as he waded into deeper water.

"Yes. I create dancers in motion and free-spirited creatures. Then I caste them in bronze putting them in permanent motion." She gave him a weak smile as if she didn't quite believe it herself. "So what do you do to relieve stress?" she said prickly.

He took off his sunglasses. Leaning in to her, he hoped to take in her scent again. She gasped as his breath lightly brushed along her neck. Unlike on the plane, he wanted her full attention. She closed her eyes for a moment and when she opened them, he scrutinized her intently. "My head and hands work together, too. I could show you how I relieve stress. However, it usually includes someone of the female persuasion." He used his artillery of charm, pushing her to see what she would do with it.

Blush tinted her cheeks. The women he kept company with wouldn't have batted an eyelash at his retort. Seeing her blush had him craving more. His cock started to come to life, which amazed him considering his intake of tequila the night before. He wanted this woman underneath him. His reaction to her was visceral. He would dive in and never come up. Those thoughts and emotions clouded his judgment and his control started to slip. God, when was the last time just talking to a woman had his body on full alert?

"Well, how do you know I want you to show me? Look around you. There are plenty of females for you to persuade." She came right back at him, challenging him with those intense blue eyes and sharp words.

He moved around uncomfortably as he tried to manage his full salute. Kitten has sass, too. Her mouth would get her into trouble, in more ways than one. This was going to get interesting. He had the devil on his shoulder. He loved a good challenge. Mystified by her response, she was a contradiction in so many ways, from her coyness to her innocent blush. He let his gaze follow down to her gorgeous, toned legs and back up to her large, supple breasts, resting on her beautifully flawless face.

He responded, "Oh, I think you want me to show you. I can tell by the shine in your eyes, the blush in your cheeks, and the way your breath makes your luscious cleavage go up and down. You're a dead giveaway. By the way, there's only one woman here I'm interested in persuading." Let the sparring begin.

Her nipples stood at attention. As her hands came up to cover them, the clay dragon slipped onto the pool deck.

He caught her hands and gently forced them in her lap. "Don't hide. I like you like this." He squeezed her hands. She sucked in her breath, which puzzled him. Why would she be surprised that he would want to look at her? He adored exquisite women. She never ceased to surprise him. The wheel of questions began to turn in his head. He'd let her off the hook this time. Glancing at her pert nipples, he picked up the dragon and examined it. "Seems like the beginnings of a dragon. Is this one to keep Eros company?" His eyebrows furrowed together. He found her fascination with dragons adorable strengthening that invisible silken cord between them. "Red dragons can represent some dark stuff, like death, anger, aggression, and danger. It can even be a warning." His tone held no amusement.

"Well, that would make sense considering what's happened lately in my life. You might say I'm at a crossroads. It's time for a new muse to help me sort through it. Maybe the danger has already passed." Her eyes were weary.

"What crossroads are you at? It sounds interesting. You like to keep me guessing." He stayed focused on her, wanting her to reveal a little more of her broken parts. What kind of danger was she in? His body went on alert, hazards of the job.

She took a deep breath. "I lost my husband about three months ago. Some things are starting to come to light that I would have liked to stay in the dark." A flash of anger crossed her face.

Leaning back, he shut his eyes briefly trying to hide his painful memory. "Saying sorry isn't enough. I know what it's like to lose someone you're close to. I lost someone, too. It was a living hell to watch, not being able to do anything about it. Sometimes, people leave behind holes." He hadn't spoken to anyone about her. Those words were long overdue. Sharing this fragment scared the shit out of him. Her death bled him like an open wound, leaving a gaping hole. Loved ones could be gone in an instant. Life could turn on a dime. He teetered between wanting to tell Marabella everything to not wanting her to see the man he had become. The one who was closed off and alone.

As she spoke her next words, he was certain he would be sharing all of it with her. He would fight through his pain to get to the other side.

"I can tell by the pain in your eyes that the person was very special to you. You're right. Sometimes, sorry isn't enough. My husband died in a suspicious car accident. No one can figure out what he was doing in Brighton Beach that time of night. As some things have come to light, I'm not sure I knew him at all." She shut her lips firmly.

Her words hit him hard. She really believed she didn't know the man she called her husband. He couldn't think of a worse betrayal. He stared at her flawless face, made up to perfection. Every lash was in place with enough blush to appear natural. The foundation and eyeliner were exact to enhance her features. He wanted to peel away the mask to reveal her. Why did she need it? He itched to know more about the workings of her.

Reaching out his hand, just like on the plane, he opened his palm to her. He wouldn't feel her energy again. That was a fluke at best. Given the current revelations about her past, he wondered if she was rolling in waves of the emotions he was so familiar with.

"What are you smiling about?" She tilted her head to peek up at him.

"I'm wondering how lightning strikes twice. What are the chances that you and I would be staying in the same place?" His eyes devoured her enticingly. The wolf to her kitten. He was one-step away from crossing the abyss into dangerous territory. He had never entertained the thought of fate. She had him questioning everything.

www.bit.ly/Truths1
www.bit.ly/Truthsnook
www.bit.ly/Truthskobo

ACKNOWLEDGMENTS

I want to thank anyone and everyone who read my book and took the time to leave a review. There are ARC readers, bloggers, reviewers, editors, cover design artists, just to name a few. Without them, books don't make in front of readers who might enjoy a good escape.

I want to thank my wonderful, patient husband who puts up with hearing about everything he didn't want to know about writing a book, including the stress.

My mother, the actress, writer, painter and drawer, continues to inspire me. She never stops learning.

Elbow, friend and sister from another lifetime, fellow writer, and PR person, write on.

Nikko, my muse, who was by my side each time I sat down to write. He didn't make it to the end of this book but his photo sits next to my computer. May he rest in peace with Koda Bear. One day, we will have two more rescues who will run our lives.

ABOUT THE AUTHOR

Kenzie lives with her husband in New England and is a huge dog lover. She has been fortunate enough to travel all over the world to places like Africa, Greece, Switzerland, Holland, France, England and, of course, Scotland. Edinburgh is one of her favorite places. It's all led to an overactive imagination. Creativity seems to be part of her soul as she paints portraits, takes photographs, and bakes. They have all added to her storytelling especially when writing about strong women and alpha men. She looks forward to adding to her adventures and her readers.

She loves to hear from her fans.
You can find her on:
Website: www.kenziemacallan.com

Sign up for her newsletter for cover reveals, news and giveaways

Facebook: www.facebook.com/kenziemacallan
Instagram: www.instagram.com/kenziemacallan
Twitter: www.twitter.com/kenzie_macallan
Pinterest: www.pinterest.com/kenziemacallan
Email: kenziemacallan@gmail.com